THE NEW SHOE

Mysteries by Arthur W. Upfield
available as Scribner Crime Classics:

THE
NEW
SHOE

Arthur W. Upfield

CHARLES SCRIBNER'S SONS

NEW YORK

CONTENTS

THE NEW SHOE

THE SPLIT POINT LIGHT

The evening sky was a true prophet. Smoky-yellow cloud fingers presented as clear a warning as the yellow-gloved hand of a traffic policeman, and all the birds obeyed the warning save the foolish one.

The cloud fingers turned to crimson, and tinted the Southern Ocean with opalescent hues. The foolish one sported with the little fish, diving and turning in the colours, and when the colours had gone and the sea mirrored the stars, he slept contentedly on the deep.

The wind came before the day, came swift and cold and strong. The day brought rain to scat upon the grey water from the grey sky, and to reveal the land far distant and shrouded in sea mist. Unlike the gulls and the gannets, the foolish one couldn't fly, but he could swim, and with frantic haste he steered for the sanctuary of the shore.

His dinner suit kept him warm for a little while and gave him buoyancy, but steadily the white horses grew in number and in strength, charging down upon him, thrusting him deep beneath their salted hooves, each one taking a little of his buoyancy before speeding onward in the race for the land. The end was as inevitable as Greek drama: the price exacted for all foolishness. He became a spent and waterlogged vessel, and the cold clamped about his valiant heart. Then lethargy quieted all his fears.

The sea surged him onward to the rocks footing the headland bearing high the Split Point Lighthouse. It failed to whiten more his shirt front, or dim the blackness of his dinner jacket, but its anger increased because its triumph was cheap and its revenge was thwarted by the currents which carried the body clear of the rocks, to deposit it at the feet of Napoleon Bonaparte.

The sea thundered its rage and the wind shrieked its fury. A gull cried with grief, and Detective Inspector Bonaparte took up the half-grown penguin, carried it above high-water mark, and buried it in the dry sand.

He thought no one was near to laugh at him.

It was late afternoon in May. The rain had been swept from the sky and the clouds were being torn to shreds by the wind which whipped the overcoat about his legs and carried the spray to sting his eyes. The one venturesome gull vanished from this place of rock and water, cliff and narrow beach, and when Bony turned his back to the sea, the wind pressed against him in effort to make him run.

Split Point is not unlike the distended claws of an angry cat's paw, forever thwarted by Eagle Rock standing safely out at sea. Bony surveyed two of these claws rising sheerly from the beach for a hundred feet or more, and then the less precipitous slope of paw rising to the base of the lighthouse. At the base of the right cliff two caves offered cold shelter, and within the rock funnel in the face of the left cliff the wind swirled grass and dead bush round and round without cease. At his low elevation, he could see all the lighthouse save its foundation upon the grassy sward, a tapering white stalk holding aloft the face of glass beneath the cardinal's red hat.

Thirty years before, Split Point Light was changed from manual to automatic control, since when it is inspected four times annually by an engineer from the Commonwealth Lighthouse and Navigation Department.

On March first, an engineer had begun his tour of inspection at nine in the morning. He found the light in perfect operation, and saw nothing to indicate anything unusual until he discovered the body of a man entombed in the thick wall.

Before nightfall that same day, the investigators from Melbourne were like ants in a piece of rotted wood. They dusted for fingerprints, and they searched high and low for the dead man's hat, his boots, and his clothes. Subsequently, they interviewed a hundred people, and scratched their heads over the result. Hope that they would swiftly draw an ace murderer from the pack dwindled till finally the only card they held was the joker.

They preserved the body in a glass tank of formalin, and scattered pictures of the dead face to every newspaper in Australia. They chivvied the crooks in Melbourne and other capital cities, and annoyed respectable folk by their questioning. Some became red with anger and others white with frustration, and in his office at Police Headquarters in Melbourne, Superintendent Bolt glared at the joker.

A day nine weeks after the engineer had found the body, Napoleon Bonaparte, on his way back to his Department in Brisbane, called on Bolt to talk about the weather. Bolt took him home and talked about a dead body no one knew, or wanted to. He admitted failure to his superior in tenacity if not in rank, and he agreed to all Bony's demands and plans for attacking this case.

Thus was the product of two races in time to bury a drowned penguin at the very foot of the now famous lighthouse, and hoping no one was laughing at him. Hope was banished.

At the edge of the cliff to his right stood a woman. She was almost directly above him. She swayed against the buffeting wind, and, did she take one step forward, she would plunge to death. She appeared to be young, and certainly was dark of hair. The grey skirt fluttered like a flag at a masthead.

It was lunacy to stand there at the edge of that weathered cliff, before her a drop of a hundred feet at least, and Bony's reaction first was of admiration for her courage, changing then to ire at the woman's stupidity. She seemed to lean against the wind, oblivious to the possibility of a sudden fall in pressure which would suck her into the gulf. He shouted up to her to draw back, but either she did not hear or, hearing, ignored the plea.

Then she slid her right foot forward to the very verge. It seemed she was going to jump. In Bony, perturbation changed to horror.

The foot was withdrawn. The woman turned a fraction, and as though from her heels there rose behind her a man. The man was shorter and more stockily built. He appeared to wrap his arms about the girl's waist, and proceeded to drag her back.

For a step or two only. She stamped her heels on his feet. She struggled to release her arms from the clamp about her waist. She exerted all her strength to drag him with her over the edge. Bony could see her frenzied face, and just discern the stony grimness on the face of the man.

Abruptly the man released her, caught her jacket with his left hand, swung her back from the cliff's edge, and neatly uppercut her. As she collapsed, he caught her again in his arms and carried her back from Bony's sight.

"Ungentlemanly, but necessary," Bony thought, and decided to make sure all had ended well.

There was no way round the eastern claw of Split Point, and no way up to the lighthouse save by walking the beach for several hundred yards the other way, crossing the bar of the inlet and negotiating the rocks which had fallen from the cliffs. As he proceeded into the inlet, the back of the headland came down to meet the level ground, and from this point he could take the long slope to the lighthouse.

The slope took Bony high above the great basin with its sand bar raised by the sea to keep the creek water within. He passed by two graves of the original pioneers of this district, on and up to skirt the eight-feet-high iron fence about the lighthouse. To his left were the houses once occupied by the keepers; to his right low clumps of tea-tree bush scattered upon the grassland to the verge of the cliffs.

The wind hissed about the corners of the iron fence; the white towering structure ignored it. On passing into the clear beyond the fence, Bony saw no one. He proceeded to the place where the girl had appeared and, keeping safely back from the cliff, was undecided what next to do. Below was the narrow strip of sand beach whereon, written plain, were his own tracks and the mark of the shallow grave he had dug with his hands. Here on the verge were the tracks of the girl's shoe heels.

There had been time for the girl and her rescuer to leave the headland by passing between the government buildings and down the opposite slope where several summer cottages were set within their hedges of lambertia. As it would be useless to search among the bush and scrub, Bony turned back from the cliff—to see a man standing a dozen yards away and calmly watching him.

He was stockily built. His face was square, and his greying hair was short and straight. He was, obviously, a permanent resident.

"Good day!" Bony said on advancing to the motionless figure.

The watcher merely nodded.

"Have you seen a young woman and a man within the last fifteen minutes?"

The man shook his head.

"How long have you been up here?" pressed Bony.

"Half an hour. Per'aps longer."

"And you've seen no one?"

"No. And if I have, what's your business with 'em?"

The box-red face was blank, but the grey eyes were hard. Bony's voice was soft.

"I was down on the beach and thought I saw a man struggling with a young woman. Were you the man?"

"No. I don't struggle with women. Good day-ee to you, mister!"

It was Bony's turn to watch as the man strode to the low crest of the headland, finally disappearing between two clumps of tea tree. He memorised those bushes, and proceeded to examine the ground.

The surface was grey and comparatively hard, but yet retained the woman's heelprints. The man's tracks were less in evidence, but he wore a boot size seven, and they were down-at-heel. The taciturn man was wearing well-conditioned boots size eight. Bony had automatically noted that.

Thus early he found himself at a slight disadvantage, for he was here as a visitor on holiday and not as an expert bush tracker. To remain in character, he must decidedly not behave as a tracker, and with casual mien he walked back to the crest and passed between the memorised bushes. Here the ground was softer. Here the ground plainly retained the tracks of boots number eight, and also boots number seven and a woman's shoes size six. All three persons were proceeding away from the cliff.

STRANGERS ARE SUSPECT!

Less than eighty miles from Melbourne, Split Point is situated between the holiday resorts of Anglesea and Lorne. Behind the point lies the inlet, and back of the inlet one can be a thousand miles from the city.

During the winter months, visitors are rare at Split Point, and at the Inlet Hotel, Bony learned he was the only guest until the next day when a Navigation Department man was expected. However, on entering the small bar he found several men who were obviously locals—soft-speaking and reserved. Their conversation ceased on his entry, and eyes examined him with an apparent lack of interest.

The licensee was large, round, bald, and beery, an incarnation of the innkeepers of Dickens's novels. His dark eyes were like those of a kookaburra, his nose a wondrous blob of blue-veined red marble.

"Go down to the beach?" he asked, drawing a glass of beer for Bony.

"Yes, Mr. Washfold. A wild afternoon, and cold. Pretty place, though. I'm going to like it."

"Looks prettier when the sun shines," returned Washfold. "Been around a bit myself, and liked no place better. You can have Melbun, all of it includin' the pubs. A shilling's my price for that hole any day."

The licensee shot a glance at the other men, received their tacit approval, and waited for opposition from this guest.

"No one living in those houses down from the lighthouse?" Bony questioned.

"Don't think. Summer houses they are. You been up there?"

"Walked up to see the lighthouse, yes."

Bony was conscious of the silence, and the licensee moved along the short bar counter to refill glasses. Then one man asked another if he had sighted the hardwood boards on order, and yet another admitted he had obtained roof guttering without much trouble. Washfold returned to Bony.

"Haven't put you down in the Lodgers' Book yet," he said. "Taking a longish spell, Mr.—er——"

"The name is Rawlings," Bony replied. "Yes, I always have a good holiday when I get my wool cheque. The wife goes to Melbourne. I clear out on my own. Good for domestic bliss, you know."

Washfold's hairless brows rose a fraction, and for the first time his beady eyes were friendly.

"In sheep, eh! My bit of wool's being sold next week. What d'you reckon? Prices hold up?"

"I think it's likely," replied Bony, pushing his glass forward. "Almost sure to now that the reserve stocks in America are low."

"That's what I was saying the other day," agreed the licensee, and Bony felt he was now beginning to be accepted. "Sheep is wool these days, Mr. Rawlings. My clip'll go into one bale. How many sheep you got?"

"Five thousand," Bony smiled. "I've five thousand sheep and no hotel, and you have a hotel and a few sheep. You're better off."

A wide grin overspread the full, round face. What the licensee would have said was prevented by the house gong announcing six o'clock and that dinner was ready.

"A drink on the house for the road," the licensee offered, and seized upon the glasses. The last drink was downed quickly, and the company filed out, Bony through the rear doorway to make for his room.

The solitary diner was waited on by the licensee's wife. Mrs. Washfold was also large and round, but her hair was thick and grey, and her eyes were large and brown. She was friendly at once, giving Bony a choice of soup and main dish. Her culinary gifts were quickly established, and her curiosity well controlled.

Bony was glad he hadn't to make polite conversation, and his mind passed over the scene in the bar and the quiet orderliness of men having a few drinks at the close of a day's work. Neither they nor the licensee evinced suspicion of him, behaving normally as men in isolated places toward the stranger.

The voice of Superintendent Bolt entered the silent dining room. "You'll find the place almost deserted. No holiday people. Few men down there on housebuilding and other contract work. Round about, and at the back of the inlet, are several farms. Prosperous farms. Wish I could park at that hotel for a fortnight. Do me. Bit of fishing—if you know where to go and when. Good tucker, and the sea air adds relish to the beer."

The "tucker" was certainly high above average. When Mrs. Washfold had left for her kitchen, the Superintendent's voice came in: heavy, easy, pleasing.

"You won't see Split Point as it was on March the first when the nude body was found in the lighthouse. On that date the place was full of visitors—people staying at their own seaside shacks, renting houses, or merely spending the day. There were twenty-seven people at the only guesthouse, and fourteen at the only pub. In addition to the visitors, there were the locals.

"I'd say that on March one there were three hundred people within two miles of that lighthouse, and today there would be a bare fifty. The trail is two months cold, and we can give you nothing to start with. Even now we can't establish the identity of the dead man. We don't know whether he was shot inside or outside the lighthouse. We haven't been able to find his clothes, and no one will own him although his picture must now be familiar to tens of thousands.

"Theories, of course, we do have. Like the armchair cops, we like to theorise. We think the dead man was a member of a gang down there for a rest, probably living in a rented house, and that a rival smoked him out and plonked him one. Right up your alley, Bony. Busman's holiday."

The Official Summary, a skeleton of a thing, was now in his suitcase. As yet he had had no opportunity to go through it and, if Bolt's assessment was correct, there was nothing much of value in it, anyway. Crafty Bolt! He knew the case Bony could never resist. And he knew, too, the fate destined for Napoleon Bonaparte should he fail to finalise this one which he, with all his experts, all his scientists, could not crack.

"No, we don't know who the victim was," said the deep and easy voice. "Don't know anything about him, and can't contact anyone who does. The dead man's prints were on the rail of the spiral staircase, and also the engineer's. No bullet marks on the walls of the lighthouse. No bloodstains. Doors locked and unlocked either with duplicate or skeleton keys. Not a thing on the body, either; not even the shoes. Fingernails tell nothing. Exceptionally little dental work done, and that a long time ago. No such thing dropped by the killer as a handkerchief nicely initialled or a gun neatly branded. She's all yours, Bony old lad: one of the best."

Wily old Bolt. The knack of putting men on their mettle had carried him high. He had relented before showing his guest to his room at one in the morning:

"It's the toughest job we've ever had to bash open, Bony, and, honestly, you think ten times about tackling it. Remember what you told me years ago? An ordinary policeman can afford to fail, but you never. The finest weight lifter that ever was didn't try to lift a pyramid. But the sun and the wind and the rain will eventually wash a pyramid away to dust, and Time may give us a hammer heavy enough to crack this nut."

The cheese was very good, so Mrs. Washfold said, and departed to bring his coffee. As he lounged at the table and sipped the coffee, he heard the voice of the boaster:

"Patience, Super, with the addition of a little intelligence, will solve any problem. I've inherited patience from my maternal forebears, and something of the intelligence of my white progenitors. Did you ever hear the story about one of Pharaoh's granaries, filled to capacity at the beginning of the seven lean years, and found empty when the disbursers went to draw grain for the starving people? No. A little mouse gnawed his way into the granary and stole one grain of wheat. He returned and stole another, and again to steal another grain of wheat—until there wasn't one grain left. Seven years it took that mouse to empty the granary. It might take me seven years to solve this lighthouse murder. Solve it I will. As recently you so aptly remarked, it's right up my alley."

The Official Mind had often ranted about his dilatoriness, and the unthinking had often claimed that any real policeman would finalise a case in half the time. He wasn't a real policeman. He had never claimed such distinction, and his Chief Commissioner in Brisbane had more than once made himself plain on this point. But the old boy had grudgingly admitted he was a hell of a good detective.

And that was the heck of a good dinner. If he wasn't careful at this Inlet Hotel, he'd grow a tummy. Nothing like a smart walk after dinner to keep lean and hard.

His shoes crunched the gravel of the short road to the highway and clip-clopped as he took the curve downward to pass the base of the headland and cross the marshland of the inlet. The stars were out, but the highway was dark, and only one having good sight could have kept to it after leaving the last of the three road lights marking the turn-in to the hotel, the café, and the Post-Office-Store. The wind was from the south, coming after him to whisper promises of triumph.

He had expected to see the light casting a straight beam in a giant circle, and he had to gaze hard toward the invisible headland before seeing the four flashes through a chink of the blackout windows to landward. Although there was no observable beam, the light could be seen by ships twenty miles away.

Ahead of him, beyond the inlet, a car came snaking down the coastal hills, its headlights probing to find the bridge across the creek. It passed Bony with singing tires, leaving him in deeper darkness. His shoes thrummed on the bridge planking, and beneath the sound they made, and seemingly beyond the noise of the car as it climbed the great curve, he fancied he heard the echo of his own feet on the road he had just left.

The wind said listen to the swans on the creek, and the swans honk-honked their awareness of him.

Bony crossed the bridge and proceeded a further half mile, when he decided to return to the fire promised by Mrs. Washfold. He was now high above the inlet, and far away were the three red stars of the distant road lights.

This road was never straight, and, even in the dark, never the same. From the top of an electric power pole a mopoke moaned at him as he passed, and later still a curlew screamed like a kurdaitcha spirit is alleged to do when after an aborigine away from his camp at night.

A car was coming down the slope on the far side of the inlet, and it seemed to dance on the flat floor of the invisible marsh. Its headlights held on the bridge as Bony neared it, and they showed a man leaning against one of the guardrails.

The car passed in a flurry of sounds, and the sounds chased it and left the bridge to the peaceful voices of the swans. Bony expected to meet the man he had seen leaning against the railing, and didn't see him until he had fallen into step at his side.

"Good night!" said the man. "Wind tendin' easterly, looks like."

"What does that foretell?" Bony asked.

"More wind before she blows out."

Face and clothes were impossible to distinguish. It was a formless bulk keeping step with him. Bony's shoes sounded sharply on the road; the feet of the other sounded dully, as though the boots were dilapidated.

"You a visitor here?" came the question in the tone of a statement.

"Yes—for a few weeks. Staying at the hotel." Silence for a dozen paces. "Are you a permanent resident at Split Point?"

"That I am. Where d'you come from?"

"I've a small place out from Swan Hill, on the Murray. Sheep. Having my annual away from the wife. You married?"

"Aye."

Another silence. The step to step was almost military in precision.

"That, apparently, is not a revolving light?" Bony presently remarked.

"That's so. Sheep, you said. What class of sheep?"

"Corriedale strain, mostly. You farm sheep?"

"Coupla hundred. Not much of a place, Split Point, for a holiday at this time of year. Better over at Lorne. More life. There's fishin' if you like it. None hereabouts. Nothing here for visitors in the winter."

"I've never been to Lorne," Bony admitted. "Fashionable, I understand—in the season."

"And out of season. More there to occupy your time. How big's your place?"

"Hundred thousand acres. On the road to Balranald."

"Out from Swan Hill! How far out?"

Bony named a small station and its position, owned by a relative of Bolt's whose name he had adopted. There appeared to be purpose behind this garrulous questioning. It was like being vetted for a Security Service job, and as they began to mount the long curve to the first of the road lights, Bony's companion asked:

"How do they call you, mister?"

"Rawlings. What's your name?"

"Rawlings," repeated the man slowly. "Rawlings, on the Balranald road out from Swan Hill. Dammit! I've passed my turnoff."

Halting abruptly, without further word he dropped back and vanished. Bony went on—listening for the other's footsteps beneath the noise of his own. He heard nothing. Having passed down this road and upward to return from the headland, he knew there was no turnoff save one at the edge of the marshland a full half mile back.

But the first of the road lights was a bare hundred yards ahead, and the voice of his walking companion was the voice of the man who had watched him at the edge of the cliff where another had wrestled with a woman.

THE CRAFTSMAN

On the plea of being tired, Bony did not long remain in the cosy bar lounge, and having mastered the contents of the Official Summary, he fell asleep with the thought that this investigation would really extend him.

He awoke at seven—one hour before the breakfast gong would be struck—and went out to the front veranda overlooking the lawn and gazed through the shelter trees at Split Point headland and the lighthouse gleaming white in the early sunlight. The air was frostily still. A blackbird probed lustily for worms, and somewhere a calf bellowed at a rooster whose crowing sounded like splintering glass.

To wait inactive one hour for a cup of tea was unthinkable—and Mrs. Washfold did look approachable. Bony walked round the outside of the building to the kitchen door, where he was met by a shaggy brown-and-white dog, a hen, and a pet sheep. Within, he saw the licensee eating breakfast.

"Good morning," Bony greeted him from outside the fly-wire door. "A king once shouted: 'My kingdom for a horse!' You hear me shout: 'My wife for a cup of tea!'"

Washfold turned and grinned a welcome.

"No deal," he said. "One woman around this joint's enough for me. Come and get it."

Bony drew open the fly-wire door and went in. The door jambed open and the dog followed him. The dog was followed by the pet sheep, and over the large, round face of Bert Washfold spread alarm. He was in time to prevent the hen entering the kitchen, and in time to shoo out the sheep and the dog, before Mrs. Washfold appeared.

"Cup of tea! Of course, Mr. Rawlings. You can get a cup of tea here any time of day or night—in the off season. Goin' to be a nice day. What's the matter with that dog, Bert?"

"Gotta flea up his nose, I suppose. Lie down, Stug. Sugar?"

"Thanks." Bony sugared his tea and drank it.

"Heavens! You'll scald your throat out!" exclaimed Mrs. Washfold. "Another cup?"

"Ah! That's better. Yes, if you please."

"And what would you like for breakfast? Cereal or porridge? And bacon and eggs or a nice fillet steak with eggs or tomatoes?"

Shafts of sunlight barred his sky-blue dressing gown, and his sleek black hair reflected the light from the door. Looking at him, the Washfolds noted the straight and slim nose, the white teeth and the blue eyes, the face barely stained with the betraying colour of his ancestry . . . and later disagreed over the ancestry. Bony bowed to Mrs. Washfold.

"Madam!" he said. "Am I in a hotel or am I at home?"

"Home," replied the licensee. "We're all at home . . . in the off season. You try out the bacon. Cured it meself. Recommend it."

"The fillet steak is also juicy," added his wife persuasively.

"And I've been urged to go and stay at Lorne," protested Bony.

"Oh! Who said that?" demanded Washfold.

"Man I met yesterday. Well-built man about fifty or so. Greying-brown hair. Grey eyes. Speaks with a faint country accent. He was wearing old clothes and old boots, and he said he owns a couple of hundred sheep."

Over the cup, Bony blandly watched these two pleasant people.

"Sounds like Tom Owen," softly stated Mrs. Washfold.

"Did he have whiskers sprouting from the bridge of his nose?" asked the large man.

"Yes," agreed Bony, and Mrs. Washfold rose to take air.

"The idea! I'll give that Tom Owen a tongue-lashin' when I see him. Lorne! Lorne's all right for the boys and girls to loll around half naked in summertime, but not all of us have figures like film stars, although you——" She blushed like a milkmaid. "Not meaning anything, Mr. Rawlings. But you know what I mean."

"Of course. And don't think I am likely to go on to Lorne. Why, with such a breakfast as you promise me, I would be foolish. Well, I must dress."

"And you get about the chores, Bert. Look at the time!"

Later, Bony followed the highway down to the inlet. The inlet was like the grass-covered bottom of a fisherman's creel, and on it the creek lay like a silver eel. Beyond the inlet, the blue sea kissed the land rising to dark-green hills. The meeting of the sea with the land extended in giant curves from headland to headland all the way to Cape Otway.

Bony was satisfied with himself and with this world. There would be no rushing about for him. As he had eaten his breakfast so would he investigate this murder . . . without an attack of indigestion. He was wholly satisfied with his preliminary moves which had brought him as a pastoralist on holiday, and having New South Wales number plates to the car he had borrowed from the Chief of the Victorian Criminal Investigation Branch, he would be able to draw nearer to backgrounds and "sense" influences withheld from known police investigators.

At the bottom of the hill he turned along a track skirting the inlet and promising to take him far into the tree-covered mountains of the hinterland.

Passing a house being constructed, he was greeted cheerily by two men tiling the roof. He met a boy driving half a dozen cows, and presently came to a neat little cottage having a low hedge guarding the small front garden. Onward he strolled to a large shedlike building of wood-slab walls and wood-slat roof. It was set back off the road, and against the front wall leaned rusting wagon tires. The large door was open, and just within, a man was industriously planing a board on a bench. His clothes were neat. His body was plump. His face was pink, and his hair was as white as the surf.

He looked up and saw Bony, who called:

"Good day-ee!"

"Good day-ee to you, sir," came the answer, and because the old man's pose was an invitation, Bony left the road and entered the building which resolved into a workshop. Wood shavings lay deep on the floor about the bench. Planks and "wads" of three- and four-ply were stacked at one end, and over near a corner was a stack of oblong boxes. The condition of the bellows behind a forge told of years which would never return.

"Great day, mister," said the craftsman.

"It is, Mr. Penwarden."

"Ah, now! How did 'e know my name?"

"The weather hasn't quite obliterated it from over your door," replied Bony. "My name is Rawlings. Staying at the hotel for a week or so. You're very busy this morning."

"Aye, I'm allus busy, Mr. Rawlings, sir." The old man's eyes were as blue and as clear as those of the dark-complexioned man who seated himself on a sawhorse and made a cigarette. He was seventy if a day, and his mind was as alert as it had been forty-odd years before. "You see, Mr. Rawlings, the Great Enemy never gives himself a spell. He rushes here and there tappin' this one on the shoulder and that one, and it 'pears to me the only way to beat him is to keep as busy as he is. He don't take notice of busy people. Haven't got the time when there's so many folk too tired to appreciate the joys of living."

"There is certainly nothing better than an occupied mind and busy hands to keep the Enemy you mentioned at bay, Mr. Penwarden." Bony knew, but he asked the question: "Have you been long in this district?"

"I built this forge and workshop pretty near sixty year ago," replied the workman. "Twenty-one I was then, and just out of me apprenticeship to a wheelwright. No motee cars and trucks them days. No flash roads to Lorne and on to Apollo Bay. Only the old track from Geelong. In summer the track was feet deep in dust, and in winter yards deep in mud."

Bony gave another cursory glance about the ancient building, ancient but still sound. Verging upon a discovery, he left the saw bench to study the wall and roof beams and rafters at closer range. The old man watched him, in his eyes an expression of enormous satisfaction, but on Bony returning to the saw bench he was working with the plane.

"You didn't drive in one nail," Bony said, almost accusingly. "All you used were wood pins, and I can't see where they were driven in."

"That's right," agreed Penwarden, proceeding to adjust the plane. "I've a flash house down the road a bit. Old woman had to have her built the year war came, and she'll be rotted out afore this shop starts to wobble in a sou'easterly gale. Houses! They build 'em with raw wood full of borers and plaster and putty and a dab or two of paint. There's mighty few jobs left these days for a real live tradesman. Me, I won't work with such trash . . . exceptin' on a certain kind of job which no one looks at for long."

"That's a beautiful board you're working on now," Bony observed. "Looks to me like red gum."

The blue eyes shone.

"Ha, ha! So you know a thing or two, eh? Thought you might when I set eyes on you. Red gum she is. I get these boards sent down special from Albury. They come from ring-barked trees on the Murray River flats, and ring-barked wood or wood killed by water will last forever. None of your three-ply veneered to look like silky oak is good enough for my special customers. One time I could give 'em teak. Now it has to be red gum, and I ain't sure I likes teak the best, neither."

26

"And what are you going to do with it?"

"Build her into a coffin. Like to see one almost done?"

"I think I would," answered Bony a trifle slowly. The coffinmaker put down his plane with care not to jar the blade and said:

"Lots of us take comfort in thinkin' we'll be lying snug when we're dead. There's graveyards and graveyards. Some is nice and dry, and some is as wet and cold as a bog. Then again, cremation is against The Book, which says that on the Last Day the bones of the dead shall be drawn together. Can't be if they're all burned up."

He turned from the bench, and Bony stood to follow him. Waving a hand contemptuously to the stack of "boxes," he went on:

"Don't look at them over there. Three-ply and gum, and tin tacks to hold 'em together. They'll give you a squint if you looks at that trash what I send to Melbourne for ten pounds apiece and are sold to the dead for fifty. Come this way, and I'll show you what a coffin should be."

Bony accompanied the carpenter to a small room and stood beside trestles set up in the centre and supporting something covered with an old and moth-eaten black velvet cloth.

"You don't see a coffin like this every day," Penwarden said as he faced his visitor above the pall. "Times is changed. People don't think about next week, tomorrow. They don't worry about being a nuisance to their relations or the state when they perish. No pride these days . . . get through work as quickly as possible for as much as possible—and refuse to do any thinkin' because thinkin' hurts."

He whisked away the cloth.

The casket was like a slab of ruby-red marble, producing the illusion of colour depth as does red wine. Save for the two plated handles either side, there was no ornamentation. The surfaces were as smooth as glass and the colour matchless.

The old man lifted the cover, watching always Bony's face to detect his reactions. Bony bent over the lid and stooped to examine the ends and the sides—and failed utterly to see the joins. The casket might have been fashioned in one piece from the heart of a tree.

Their gaze clashed, and as the old man closed the lid the air faintly hissed at the final compression. Again he raised and closed the lid, and again there was the sound of air being caught in a trap. The lid was raised yet again and poised on the side to which it was hinged, and Bony bent to see into the interior and to note the curved floor to take the back and the curved rest for the neck. Finally he stood away and gazed at the coffinmaker without speaking.

"Inside is only the natural gloss," Penwarden said. "I do a lot to the outside to bring up that colour in the wood. Nothing wrong with her to sleep in for a long time, is there?"

"Nothing," softly agreed Bony.

Penwarden caressed the lid before closing it, and his hands fluttered like butterflies as he wiped away the finger marks and drew the cover over the casket.

"Got two like it at home," he said, cheerfully. "One for me, and t'other for the old woman. They rest under the bed. Our shrouds are in 'em, too. Now and then the old woman opens 'em up and airs the shrouds and pops a bit of lavender in. My father and mother had their coffins waitin' for 'em, and my grandfather brought hisn with him on the ship from England. Ah yes, times is changed, but us Penwardens don't change, and there's others what don't change, neither."

"They must be rare, these people," Bony commented when following the craftsman back to his bench.

"You say true, Mr. Rawlings, sir, you say true. And gettin' rarer."

"How long does it occupy to make a coffin like that in the other room?"

"Well, it would be guessing. I don't work on one continuous. Tallying the time, I suppose it'd take me thirty ten-hour days . . . I must have begun that one three months back. You see, there's them other jobs to slap up with glue and tacks. I'm always behind orders with them."

"And the cost?"

"Depends," replied the old man, and the note in his voice barred further questioning on this angle.

Pensively, Bony watched the plane glide to and fro along the red-gum board, and the shavings which fell to the floor already deep with shavings were wafer thin. The overlong white hair tended to obscure the workman's vision, and now and then he would toss back his head. The bare arms were fatless and hard; the legs encased by drill were sturdy and strong. Bony wanted to ask how old Penwarden was, and remembered he had said he had built the shop when twenty-one nearly sixty years ago. From the firm throat issued a deep chuckle.

"Got to fit me special customers, you know. Generally takes a fittin' afore I puts the boards together, and then again just after I lays the bed to make the lying nice and comfortable. Nothing worse than an uncomfortable coffin you have to lie in for years and years maybe. That casket inside is for Mrs. Owen. She be getting on, too, and for years wouldn't have no coffin to lie alongside Tom's under the bed. Took him a time to persuade her to take a first fitting. Then one day he brings her along, and we talk and talk, persuadin' her to lie atween the boards I just leaned together, sort of. Got her legs straight at last, and her arms nice and cosy, and I'm making me marks when up she jumps screeching like a hen what's laid her first egg. Took Tom a long time to quiet her down, and my old woman had to lend him a hand. Now we're waitin' for the final fitting, but we don't have no hope of getting her again."

Bony was quite sure that no amount of persuasion would induce him to "take" a fitting, and he said:

"Old English name, Penwarden, isn't it? Cornish?"

"Devonshire, me father came from. There's people here called Wessex. That goes way back. Used to be a part of England called Wessex. Had its kings, too. This local Wessex was born here. His father took up land in them hills back of the inlet. The Owens lives this side of the Wessexes. Dearie me! The Lord blesses some and thrashes t'others. He blessed the Owens and thrashed the Wessexes, and with us Penwardens He seemed to take turn and turn about."

The plane was placed carefully away, and the coat was taken from the nail in the wall at the end of the bench.

"Time for grub," announced the old man. "Staying up at the hotel, eh? Sound people, the Washfolds. Ain't been there long, but they're sound."

"Thank you for being so neighbourly, Mr. Penwarden," Bony told him. "I've really enjoyed talking with you and viewing your work."

29

"Tain't nothin', Mr. Rawlings, sir. Come along again sometime. Allus glad to see you."

Bony strolled back to the hotel, undecided whether to chuckle or to be horrified by the picture of Mrs. Owen undergoing the trial of being fitted.

THE GLASS JEWEL

Bony found a tall and weathered man seated at his luncheon table. Mrs. Washfold bustled in to introduce them.

"This is Mr. Fisher from the Navigation Department," she said. "Going to work at the lighthouse. Thought you two might like to sit together. Meet Mr. Rawlings, Mr. Fisher."

"Working at the lighthouse, eh!" exclaimed Bony. "I'd like to go over it."

"Any time you like," assented the engineer. "I'm startin' work about two. Walk right in. I'll leave the door open for you."

"You take them steps easy, Mr. Rawlings," interposed the licensee's wife. "There's about a hundred and twenty of 'em, so they say, and when you're not used to it the climb will make your legs ache that much you won't get no sleep for nights. A little vegetable soup, now?"

It was easy and quite natural, and every time Mrs. Washfold appeared they were talking about coastal lights and of Fisher's experiences in many of them.

Toward three o'clock Bony left the private entrance and at once was joined by the hotel dog. Stug, it was called, and when Bony had asked for the meaning, he was advised to reverse the letters. The name, in reverse, was well chosen in view of the animal's condition. He wanted to be acknowledged and greatly appreciated Bony's attention.

With the dog, who kept with him all the way, its interest in this new friend never obscured by the alluring scents it came across, Bony arrived at the gate in the lighthouse fence, paused to examine visually the heavy padlock attached to the chain, and passed inside, closing the gate after him and the dog. Within the enclosure stood a forge and bags of fuel, and to one side against the iron fence was a lean-to shed.

The fence, the yard, himself, and the dog were, of course, dwarfed by the mighty structure towering to the cloud-flecked sky. On glancing upward, the overhanging balcony prevented him from sighting the windows of the light and the red dome surmounting it. It had been painted recently, and Bony wondered how the painters had done their work.

The yard interested him particularly, and for one purpose. Whereas above-surface objects, such as the forge and the shed, might have interested the city detective, it was the ground which automatically claimed this man's attention.

Since the last of the police investigators had been here rain had wiped clean the ground within this yard, and since the rain had fallen there was one set of footprints between the fence gate and the lighthouse door. Obviously they had been left by Fisher.

The lighthouse door was open, and on entering the building, Bony found himself in a narrow chamber flanked by rows of tall steel gas cylinders. Beyond this small chamber was the bottom of the spiral staircase, and on the bottom step sat Fisher.

"Ah, there you are, Fisher," Bony said, and drew forward an empty case to sit with him. "Don't move. I'll smoke a cigarette and we'll talk before going up. How's the leg?"

"The leg, Inspector! All right. How did you know I'd damaged my hip a few years ago?"

"Little bird. Right hip, wasn't it? Caused a limp."

"Yes, it did. But I don't limp now."

"Just a little. Spent most of your time at sea?"

"That's so. All us lighthouse men have been seamen in our time."

"Well now, let's get to work. First, you played your part well at lunch. Superintendent Bolt talked to you?"

"Yes, Inspector. Told me not to give you away as a detective."

"Then forget I am one, and remember that my name is Rawlings —that I'm a sheepman. Are you the man who found the body?"

"Yes. It was crook because I wasn't thinkin' of the naked and the dead. I was thinkin' of sun valves at the time." A humourless chuckle rose from the vicinity of the man's belt. "Bodies in light-houses aren't so thick as daisies in a paddock. I walked in here to do a job to one of the spare cylinder connections, and I found the sun valve——"

"Wait. We'll come to that. I understand you have been with your Department for nine years. You would know the routine. This lighthouse is inspected four times annually, is it not?"

"Yes, as near as possible in the first week in February, May, August, and November each year. It happens that this is inspection time. In fact, Superintendent Bolt only just told me in time about you being here. I was due the day after tomorrow."

"Did you inspect the light in February, the usual routine time?"

"Yes."

"Then your visit here on March the first was not a routine visit?"

"No, it wasn't. When I was down here early in February, I couldn't finish a job, so I fixed it up pro tem and reported to the office that it might last all right until the next inspection. The office said it should be looked at before then, and that's why I was sent down three weeks later to fix it properly."

"Anyone outside your office know you were coming?"

"No."

"Therefore, anyone familiar with the inspection periods would not anticipate anyone coming here again till early in May? Many local people know the inspection periods?"

"All of 'em would know."

"Apparently the police did not know it," Bony said, and Fisher caught the note of satisfaction. "They understand you came here on a routine inspection."

"Well, they asked me why I came down, and I told 'em I came on inspection duty. That's what I am—engineer-inspector of automatic coast lights."

"Ah, I can see where the slight discrepancy occurred. Don't worry about the matter, now we have it clear. Let me look at the keys."

Fisher produced a bunch of keys and selected one which fitted the yard-gate padlock and another which fitted the lock in the light-house door. Both keys could quite easily be duplicated. Without comment, Bony returned them.

"I assume you Navigation men have to know several trades," he said.

"That's so, Inspector. Rigging and welding and the like. Have to be used to heights, too. The d.s. seemed to have an idea that a Navigation Department man could have done the murder. They checked up on us all pretty thoroughly."

"Matter of work," murmured Bony. "Now show me over. I want you to proceed exactly as you did when you came here in March, beginning from where you opened the door and ending at that place where you found the body. I am not questioning your statement made to the detectives: it will be to my own advantage to follow you on the course you took that morning."

Fisher stood with Bony.

"When I opened the door," he said, "the first thing I did was smell for escaping gas, and then I looked at the pressure gauges on the cylinders and saw that the pressure was o.k. You see, although I had that special job to complete, the ordinary inspection had to be done even though I'd done it three weeks before. So I ran an eye over the cocks and connections down here and then I went on up."

He proceeded to mount the stairway, Bony following. Their shoes rang metallically on the iron steps centred to the spiralling iron handrail. Thirty-one steps brought them to the first landing, occupying a half-circle. It was almost dark, the handrail gleaming like pewter in the faint light thrown up from the bottom and passed down from the distant upper floor.

A further series of thirty-one steps brought them to another landing, and Bony's thigh muscles were beginning to complain. On reaching the third landing, he was thankful he hadn't five hundred steps to mount, and after leaving this landing the light rapidly became stronger till they reached the top floor.

They were now at the summit of the main stone-and-cement structure upon which rested the cupola housing the light. To reach the light was a further flight of fifteen-odd steps, and a steel gangway circled the light similar to that from which a ship's engine is serviced. The engineer went up, and Bony followed.

The daylight entering through the outside plain glass "face" of the lighthouse illumined the shell of prisms, making of them a jewel deserving the softest plush for background. The beauty entranced Bony, so entirely unexpected was it.

In the centre of the prisms and almost at their base nestled a cluster of ordinary acetylene-gas jets, and in the heart of the cluster lay another burning a tiny light. The engineer turned a small cock outside the prisms, and the cluster of jets flamed, magnifying the light to ten thousand candle power. The light went out, then flamed again. There was an eclipse, and this was followed by four flashes covering a period of twelve seconds prior to the next eclipse.

Bony found the engineer watching him, and he nodded, whereupon Fisher turned the cock and the flashing lights ended.

"Having tested the light," he said, "I went outside to take a look at the sun valve, not that there could be anything wrong with it, because the jets were operating."

Bony followed him down to the main floor, and Fisher opened a door in the circling iron wall and passed outside. Bony followed, finding himself on the narrow steel balcony, and at once thought of how much the policeman suffers to maintain law and order.

He closed his eyes and held tightly to the railing of the spidery balcony. The narrow overhanging of ledge beneath prevented anyone from looking directly down the white wall, and not for several moments did he ascertain that fact for himself. On opening his eyes, he gazed determinedly out over the inlet to the mountains, and then at the highway and the bridge where the man Owen had waited for him.

He followed Fisher round the balcony, and there was nothing other than the blue and shadowed sea, until he ventured to look down and courageously gazed upon the paw and the wide talons of Split Point. The whitewashed rocks and the sandy beach seemed not half a dozen feet below the edge of the headland.

"Long way down," said the engineer, and Bony turned to look at him. The man's eyes were dark and seemed full of meaning. The hands resting on the cobweb of balcony rail were like the hands of a giant. For them to pick up a man and toss him over would require no great effort. Bony decided he had never really adored heights.

They passed on round the balcony, and when Fisher again

stopped, he reached up and touched a cylinder of glass about twelve inches long and metal-capped at both ends.

"This is the sun valve," he explained. "The mechanics are simple when you know. The interior is extremely sensitive to light, but the light must contain heat. Sunlight contains heat, moonlight doesn't. When the sun rises, no matter what clouds there are, its light acts on the valve and the valve automatically turns off the supply of gas to the jets, and when the sun goes down, the gas is automatically turned on again. The pilot light in the middle of the jets is a permanent light, and the mechanism operating the jets to make them flash is another piece of mechanism.

"Now I came out here to take a look at the sun valve, as usual, and I found the glass was cracked. Can't make out what cracked it. Anyway, it was cracked, and I went inside for my bag of tools and took it off, intending to take it back to Melbourne, and knowing there was a spare valve down below."

"All right. I'll follow you," Bony said, slightly impatient to get off that balcony.

He was glad to be inside again, and see Fisher close the iron door and bar it. Once he glanced upward at the jewel set in steel, and then proceeded to follow the engineer down the spiralling steps.

Just before they came to the lowest landing, Fisher stopped and switched on a flashlight, waiting for Bony to stand with him. He then opened a door in the wall to reveal a cavity approximately four feet thick and four by four feet high and wide.

"There used to be a window on the outside of this chamber," he said. "Before the light was automatic, the red danger lamp was installed here, and because nothing was done with the space after the lamp was removed, the foreman of a repair gang made the door to fit so that the place could be used as a locker for spare parts.

"The spare sun valve was kept here. I opened the door, and even put my hand inside for the valve. Then I switched on the torch and saw it. Not the sun valve. I thought it was a sort of octopus. My torch beam was aimed straight at the face, and the eyes were wide open and the mouth was sagging. I hadn't sort of expected to see that."

"Certainly unlikely," Bony said dryly. "It must have hit you hard."

"It did so," agreed Fisher. "How I went down to the bottom I don't recollect. Could have been headfirst. I was down and out of this lighthouse in two ticks, and even now I don't like coming back to it, or stopping here by this locker."

"Then let us go on down."

It was dark when the engineer switched off his light.

"Thought we left the door open," he said, turning on the torch. "Didn't you?"

"We did," assented Bony. "Actually, I left it open before sitting on the case and making a cigarette. Wind must have blown it shut."

"Not likely. Too heavy."

The door hinges were certainly too resistant for the slight wind to move the heavy door. The dog waited in the yard, and he was panting. Bony saw that the yard gate was shut as he had left it, and saw, too, that between the entrance to the lighthouse and the yard gate there was a third set of footprints made by a man's shoes. Watched curiously by Fisher, he sauntered to the gate without letting the engineer know he was gazing at those prints which here and there overlay their own. He opened the gate and looked out, saw no one, and closed it again.

Whilst they had been up to the light, someone had come in and gone from the yard. The person had been wearing a man's shoes that were either a small seven or a large six, and the peculiar item in the story told by the footprints was that the maker of them had come and gone on tiptoe. Peculiar because the ground was soft and even a horse could have walked about the yard without anyone inside the lighthouse hearing it.

NOT IN THE SUMMARY

As Mrs. Washfold had warned, the climb to the light had not been without cost to his legs. Complaining muscles had some influence on his decision to give up tracking the person in small shoes or boots who, on emerging from the fence gate, had walked away across the tough headland grass. He would remember those tracks and recognise them again did he see them a year hence.

Part way down the headland to the inlet was a seat, and here Bony rolled a cigarette and gently pushed Stug from sitting on his foot to scratch for fleas. The old dog took the hint and lay down to rest his muzzle on his paws and watch him in canine infatuation.

"Strange goings on, Stug, I must say," Bony commented. "Friend of yours, without doubt, a friend who walks about on tiptoe when doing so is entirely unnecessary, a friend who stands firm on the ground just outside the lighthouse door. Slightly pigeon-toed is that friend of yours. Could be a jockey, you know. Jockeys are small men, and all horsemen are slightly pigeon-toed. Well, well. We'll pick him up sometime."

The hump of the headland partially protected man and dog from the south wind, cold and tangy. The sun was low above distant mountains back of Lorne, and Bony decided that the slight elevation above the inlet was preferable to that balcony where Fisher was now cleaning windows.

The fact that Fisher had come down from Melbourne to complete work left undone at the previous routine inspection was a distinct and vital omission in the Official Summary of this case.

Although Bolt had said there was no proof of the victim having been shot inside or outside the lighthouse, there was firm support for the theory that the murder had been committed inside because the victim's fingerprints were on the handrail of the staircase.

It was, of course, obvious that the killer had easy access to the lighthouse. The gate padlock and the lighthouse door lock were both old-fashioned, simple, and strong. They had been examined by experts who stated that neither had been "picked" and that if the actual keys had not been illegally used, then either duplicates or skeleton keys had been.

The official opinion was that the murderer or the victim or both were familiar with the Split Point Lighthouse and thus were permanent or local residents, and that the murderer knew the approximate date of the next lighthouse inspection. He had pushed the body into the locker, hoping to gain more time than he could expect had he left it on the steps. Thus the killer anticipated that the body would remain undiscovered at shortest two months. Unusual circumstances brought discovery within twenty-four hours.

As Bony himself observed, no one without knowledge of the locker could possibly see the door when passing up or down the steps, and such was the colouring of the door against the surrounding wall it was doubtful that, even with a flashlight, a stranger would see it.

The locker had been contrived but a few weeks prior to the previous Christmas by the Repair Gang, three specialists who are sent far and wide to renovate both automatic and manual lighthouses. Like Fisher, these specialists had been in the Department's employ for many years, and, as Fisher had mentioned, they had, with himself, been thoroughly vetted by Bolt's team.

"Looks to me, Stug, as though the gentleman who interests us is one of the lighthouse men," Bony observed to the dog. "But according to the Summary, every one of them is not only of excellent repute but has no connection with anyone locally. And further to confuse the old mind, Fisher said that every local resident would know the approximate date of the periodic inspections. Question: 'Would any local resident know about that locker?'

"Making that locker would not be of such importance in the minds of the Repair Gang, even to mention it outside themselves. Maybe, whilst they were working there, someone called and asked to go up to the light, saw them working on the locker, noted its situation, and eventually decided to use it. The gate and door locks would not hinder a burglar serving his apprenticeship. Yet the Repair Gang told the police that whilst at work here, no one went up to see the light. No one asked for permission, which would have been given."

The identity of the victim stopped short at the description of the body and broadcast by the press, together with pictures. He was judged to be between forty and forty-five. He was five feet eleven inches, and weighed within a pound of eleven stone. His foot size was seven, his collar size fifteen, and his hat size was six and one half. His eyes were hazel, his hair light brown and wavy. The only distinguishing mark was a mole between the shoulder blades. A number of persons were permitted to view the body in the formalin tank, but no one had identified it.

"There must be someone," argued Bolt, "someone other than the murderer, who could identify our body. No one can be so isolated as not to impress his image on the mind of at least one person. This unfortunate could not fail to be remembered by someone."

The man had been shot with an ordinary .32 bullet fired from a revolver. The bullet had shattered the heart and lodged in the spine, and the angle proved that the killer had stood higher than the victim. The assumption that the crime had been committed inside the lighthouse was thus strengthened by the theory that the murderer was standing higher on the spiral steps when he fired.

From these meagre facts, how to make a start? Not from the body, which no one could identify. Not from the clothes, which could not be found. Not from the scene of the murder, for that could not be accurately established. There was blood on the body about the wound and about the sagging mouth, but none on the steps or the wall of the lighthouse. The absence of blood within the locker indicated only that the bleeding had stopped prior to the entombment.

"Now they expect me to direct light on all this confusion and within an hour or so tell them who did it and why, and where to find the guilty person," Bony told Stug. "Fisher reports his find, and the uniformed police arrive and proceed to tramp in and out like blowflies through a hole in a meat safe. Teamwork they call it, Stug. They then rush out down to the pub for drinks, and to the first person they come across they say: 'Hey, you!' And that first person shrinks into his shell and goes dumb. I don't blame him.

"Tomorrow, or the next day, I'll probably receive a note saying my seconding to Victoria is to be for a week or ten days, and I shall be subjected to other annoyances reminding me that I am a servant of a damned Government Department, and pointing out that if I do not pull my forelock I shall be sacked and my wife and children will starve.

"Solve this small problem! Of course, Stug, we'll solve it. In our own good time, not the bosses' time. It's been pleasant sitting here, and now the sun is about to set and in the bar of the Inlet Hotel men will be drinking. And where men drink, one learns. When men drink, one learns quickly."

What a case! What a place for what a case! The sea air caused his eyes to be heavy as though with lack of sleep, and he swung down sharply to the picnic ground and thence to the highway with no thought of his leg muscles until he began to mount the slope to the hotel.

As far removed as Mars was Melbourne and Bolt and crime and criminals, and even farther away was Brisbane where dwelt the ogre calling himself Colonel Spender. It was good to be alive, to recall that he had never yet failed either his superiors or himself, especially himself. Despite his aching legs, he walked with the litheness of youth.

Outside the bar stood a large truck loaded with firewood. Inside were two men drinking beer served by Mrs. Washfold. It was yet a trifle early for the housebuilders. When Bony entered, Stug squatted on the door mat.

"Hullo, Mr. Rawlings!" greeted the licensee's wife. "What did you think of our lighthouse? Tried your legs, I bet."

"Just a trifle, Mrs. Washfold."

Dressed in black, her cubic proportions made the small section behind the bar barely large enough to contain her. She had made no attempt to put on her face, which shone from the application of soap. The smile she tendered to Bony held no guile, and with him it accepted the two men.

One of these was slightly above six feet, well built, weathered to the tint of red ochre which the blacks discovered in South Australia. The other was short, rotund, agile, and his complexion was darker than Bony's. Both were about the same age—thirty. The eyes of both were grey. Bony enquiringly raised his brows.

"Take a drink with me?" he suggested.

"Don't mind if I do," replied the tall man.

The other smiled, and the smile was slow and sure.

"Me, I'll take a drink with anyone. You go up to the light?"

"Course Mr. Rawlings went up," interposed Mrs. Washfold. "I seen him on the balcony with the engineer. I wouldn't have been there for a hundred quid." She set the glasses before them. "Wouldn't go up there again for a thousand."

"For a thousand quid I'd go up to the top of the dome and stand on me head," said the tall man.

"And I," added the other, giving that slow smile, "I'd go with you and hold your feet up. For a thousand quid I'd do anything. Luck!"

They drank. Bony would have "shouted" again but for the quiet air of independence of these men, the taller of whom asked:

"Didn't see a body in that locker, I suppose?"

"No," Bony answered. "I went up to see the light. In its way a beautiful setting. I read about the murder, of course, but I was much more interested in the lighthouse."

"That murder was a funny business," stated the tall man, and his companion looked at him, smiling as though waiting for a joke. "Neat, that's what it was. I must say I like a good murder."

The smile on the face of his mate broadened, seemingly created more by affection than by humour. Mrs. Washfold's voice was acid.

"I don't, Moss, and I'm sure Mr. Rawlings don't, either."

"It's certainly remarkable that no one can identify the victim," Bony said soothingly. "He must have been a casual visitor. A local man would have been missed."

"Yair," the short man agreed, and to Mrs. Washfold: "Eric told me that him and all the other drivers was taken up to Melbun to have a deck at the corpse. None of 'em could remember seeing the bloke on their run."

"Eric! Who's he?" casually asked Bony.

"Drives one of the buses between Lorne and Geelong."

"You must have been busy at that time, Mrs. Washfold," Bony said, and the woman in black thrust out her chin.

"Fourteen guests and half a dozen or more detectives. The Chief of the C.I.B. was one, and Inspector Snook another. Didn't have no time for the Inspector, but the Superintendent was a real gent. They musta been disappointed at getting nowhere."

"Aw, don't be too sure they're getting nowhere," objected the tall man. "They don't let out all they know, and they never let up, neither. Remember the Pyjamas Girl case. Went on for years, and then a cop."

"Yes, and then what?" snapped Mrs. Washfold. "Found him guilty, and gave him a year or two in gaol, and then worked him out of the country and back to his own. Paid his fare, too."

The rear door opened and the licensee appeared. He paused to take in the empty glasses, forgotten by the absorbed Mrs. Washfold and the men interested in her words. When he joined his wife, there wasn't turning room behind the counter.

"Dry argument," he snorted. "What are we waitin' for?" Pouncing on the glasses, he filled them.

"I was sayin'," remarked the tall man, "that the police'll get the bloke what done this lighthouse murder . . . tomorrer, the next day, sometime. Betcher."

"Zac," offered his mate, and smiled at Bony. "What's the worry, any ow?"

"Betcher a quid the police finds the murderer," persisted the other.

"A fiver," raised the short man, and dragged a roll from his hip pocket.

"A fiver! All right, a fiver," agreed the other, and also produced a roll.

"Cobbers' agreement," said the short man, and shoved the roll back into his pocket.

"Cobbers' agreement it is," said the tall man, doing likewise.

Washfold leaned over the counter toward Bony.

"Plenty of money, eh?" he remarked loudly. "The downtrodden workingmen. The capitalist-starved workingmen. And you and me, Mr. Rawlings, has to slave our hearts out to support big, loafin', hungry wives what'll let the dinner spoil sooner than tend to it. All right, Dick Lake, you can shout. And then, Moss, you next."

"Suits me," replied the short man, again smiling. The old felt hat was perched at the back of his fair head, and the smile had become a fixture. Mrs. Washfold edged herself through the counter flap to reach the rear door, and Dick Lake caught her arm, saying: "Stay here with us, and we'll make the old man sweat pulling the beer. Bet I can drink more beer than you."

"I'm not takin' you on, Dick Lake," replied the woman, both pleasure and indignation in her voice.

"Aw, have a heart, Mrs. Washfold. Be a sport. About a couple more and I'll be flat out."

"I'll have one drink with you boys, and no more. I've the dinner to serve up."

"Worst pub I ever been in. No friendliness. No sport. Make it a long one, Bert."

The other man, addressed as Moss Way, joined Bony.

"Didn't you look into that locker?" he asked hopefully.

"Well, the engineer did show it to me," conceded Bony. "But I really didn't want to look into it, you know."

"Cripes, you lost a chance. Hey, Dick. What's that locker like? You worked with the Repair Gang when they was down before Christmas. How big's it?"

Lake turned from talking to Mrs. Washfold.

"Just a hole in the ruddy wall. Bit above the first landin'. There was a winder, and they used to put the danger lamp there. The foreman cemented the winder and fixed a door to make her a cupboard for spare parts."

"How big?" pressed the tall man.

"Four be four be four. Big enough to take a naked man, anyhow."

"You were in the Navigation Department?" remarked Bony.

"Me? Never. I was took on as a casual hand when the gang was here. Good job. Good wages. Funny thing was that I got six and tenpence a week more'n the tradesmen, and they had to do all the high climbing. They reckon a wharf labourer gets more than a university professor, and they're about right."

"Any other casuals beside you?"

"Nope. Only me. I'm enough. You stayin' here for a spell?"

"Staying here for several weeks," interjected Mrs. Washfold.

"What we're not doing," declared the tall man, and the short one smiled at Bony, and at Mrs. Washfold, and suffered himself to be led out to the truck.

Mrs. Washfold slipped away to the kitchen. Her husband proceeded to tell Bony that Dick Lake and Moss Way were a couple of characters and were partners in a wood-carting-general-carrier business. Bony listened with one ear. No mention was made in the Summary of any casual hand employed in the Repair Gang.

Fisher appeared with three of the housebuilders, and there was time for a round of drinks before Mrs. Washfold beat the dinner gong and her husband shouted: "Six o'clock, gents!"

At dinner Bony told Fisher he could return to Melbourne, leaving the keys of the lighthouse with him.

CASKETS ON OFFER

At the close of his first week at Split Point, Bony was liking the place with the quiet satisfaction of the man who prefers a seascape to a surrealist nightmare, Dickens to Superman. In Melbourne, Superintendent Bolt wondered how he was making out, and away up in Brisbane the Queensland Chief Commissioner, Colonel Spender, was demanding to know—one, what the hell did that damned Bonaparte think he was doing by mooning around Victoria and, two, why the hell did he ever agree to the seconding of his pet officer to another state?

Bony was unconscious of Time and the necessity of Results. He sat on a bench and watched old Penwarden working with cheap wood on coffins to be sent to undertakers in Melbourne. It seemed certain that the old man would live and be active for another thirty years and that Bony himself was destined to reach the century. These two ignored Time. Ever had they refused to be bustled, to be annoyed by Authority, to be daunted by Life. Bony found affinity with Penwarden, who had lived from one age into another and refused to permit the last to erase the influences of the first.

At his third visit to the old wheelwright-cum-coffinmaker, Bony asked permission to look again upon the casket built for Mrs. Tom Owen, and, permission being granted, he retired to the small annex and lifted the cloth and stood enraptured by the loveliness of man's handicraft. When the old man joined him, he had raised the cover and was standing a little back from it to observe how the light appeared to penetrate deep below the surface, and quietly the old man said:

"Life is a Forge. Sorrow is the Fire and Pain the Hammer. Comes Death to cool the Vessel. Like to try her out?"

Old Penwarden stood with his finger tips resting on the edge of one side panel, and, regarding him, Bony realised that he was being most specially favoured. Said the old man:

"You'd fit nicely. Take off your shoes . . . might scratch."

He saw the light gleam in Bony's eyes, witnessed the momentary hesitation before succumbing to the invitation. Bony removed his shoes and climbed into the casket and laid himself within. He felt the curving wood caressing his spine and shoulders. He felt the rest against his neck. There was no discomfort, lying there, and he looked up into the bright blue eyes expectantly regarding him.

"I couldn't be more comfortable in bed," he said, and with effort made haste slowly to sit up and climb out.

"You wouldn't like to try her with the lid down?" was the hopeful suggestion.

"Well, er . . ."

The old man chuckled and combed back his white hair with callused fingers.

"With the lid down you wouldn't see a blink o' light—not like some of the boxes I've seen made of pine and suchlike. Same with the houses they build these days."

"Mrs. Owen not had her second fitting yet?"

Old Penwarden chortled and his blue eyes were full of laughter.

"She be a frightened one that," he said. "About your size and shape exceptin' across the hips." He patted the casket with his left hand, and with the cloth in his right polished out the hand marks they had left on the cover. "Getting you to try her will have to do. You found her comfortable enough, you said. Said she fitted into the small of the back and across the shoulders. Reckon I'll tell Owen she'll do without the second fitting."

"Owen has his casket, I think you mentioned," Bony remarked, and refrained from laughing.

"Too right, he has. I made hisn back in '29. Made one for Eli

45

Wessex and another for Eli's old woman afore the 1914 war. Them's of teak and they ain't so colorful as this red gum."

"There's a daughter, isn't there? Made one for her?"

"Mary Wessex! Naw. Too young she be, for one thing, and for another . . . Well, you see, Mr. Rawlings, sir, people have to be grow'd steady and settled, a sort of part of their surroundings. A young gal wants a glory box, not a coffin. I made Mary a glory box outa silky oak from Queensland. She was goin' to marry a lad up Geelong way, but he went away to the war and was killed."

"That was sad for her," Bony interposed.

" 'Twas so. Took it to heart too much and for too long. Her brother went to the war, too. Eldred Wessex didn't come home, either. Wasn't killed, or anything like that, mind you. Just didn't come home after the war, but went off to Amerikee."

The woodworker took a sight along the edge of a board. In the white gum outside a kookaburra cackled and raised a laugh from its mate farther away. A motor on the highway laboured up the rise towards the Post Office. Carrying the board under an arm, the old man led the way back to the planing bench.

"You've heard about our murder, I suppose," he asked, and the abrupt switch of subject caused Bony mentally to blink.

"Yes, of course."

"Very mysterious, that was. No one about here never before set eyes on the man in the lighthouse. Seems to have put the police well ashore, don't it?"

"That's so. Did you see the dead man?"

"I did. The superintendent came along and asked me to look at him, saying as how I'd been here so long I might know him. But I didn't. Never seen him. No one here had ever seen him, either. Musta been brought from a distance, or might have been just a summer visitor. Pity that happened. Gives the place a bad name. Couldn't have happened if the keepers had been there."

"The light was changed to automatic some thirty-odd years ago, I understand. You've been up to the light, I suppose?"

"Been up it? Several times when I was younger than I am now. Mighty peculiar no one come forward to say who the dead man was. Picture in the papers an' all. Someone must know him."

"I suppose it's possible he could have been killed in one of the many summer cottages in this district," surmised Bony.

"That's likely what happened," agreed the old man. "But then a lot of things could have happened which for us don't make sense."

"What seems so extraordinary is how the victim or the murderer was able to get into the lighthouse," Bony murmured. "The keys are always kept in Melbourne, so the engineer said."

Penwarden settled the board on the bench to his satisfaction and took up a plane.

"Them lighthouse locks could be turned with skeleton keys. The padlock to this shop door is a skeleton. I made her three years back when I lost the proper one. The lighthouse locks ain't nothing from the ordinary." The plane went to work and the shavings rolled and twisted away from it to fall to the littered floor. Bony went back to the subject of rented houses.

Yes, it was quite likely that the owner of such a house could let it to a person he would never see, the arrangement being conducted through the post. This line of enquiry added to rather than subtracted from the difficulties confronting him, and in any case it had been thoroughly explored by Bolt's team as well as the local men.

"The lighthouse has never provided much work for people in this district, I suppose," he said, idly regarding the grain in the wood shavings falling from the plane.

"Not since she was built," replied the old man. "They put on casual labour sometimes when the Repair Gang comes down from Melbourne. Young Dick Lake got a job there last year. Lasted a few weeks."

"That was when the Gang made a locker from the old red lamp bay, wasn't it?"

"That's so."

"So you know about that?"

"About making that locker? Yes. 'Tain't much we don't get to hear about. The feller that put the body in there musta known about that new locker, too."

"It would seem certain. And was also in possession of skeleton keys."

The worker stopped to stare at his visitor.

47

"That's so," he agreed. "Or they musta took impressions of the lighthouse keys to have got in."

"They! D'you think there were more than one in the killing?"

Blue eyes clashed with blue eyes. Bony's gaze held the longer. The old man bent over his plane and thrust and thrust.

"Maybe," he said. "I don't know. Could have been more'n one in it. 'Tain't much use us talking about it. We only goes round in circles. Putting the dead man in that locker don't make no sense to me, and I allus say that what don't make sense ain't worth worrying about. Let them worry what's paid to. Murder always will out some time or another. And then there's a load of sorrow slid into innocent hearts, and the sun don't shine no more."

The white wood shavings continued to spill over to the floor and lay atop shavings of red wood, and Bony picked up a red shaving to compare the grain with that of the white wood. Into the peaceful silence, which seemed more of the mind than of this quiet corner of the world, crept the noise of a motor. The noise outraged the silence, and was swiftly slain. They heard men's voices and there appeared the wood carters.

"Good day-ee, Ed!" exclaimed Moss Way.

"How do!" supplemented the younger, Dick Lake, nodding perkily to Bony. "You gonna buy a box for yourself?"

"You produce an idea," replied Bony smilingly, and the younger man nodded towards the adjacent room, saying:

"The one in there's a beaut. Seen 'er?"

"Mr. Rawlings has seen that casket," interrupted old Penwarden, faintly stern. "What d'you two want?"

"Nuthin'," answered Lake, his face widened by his smile. "Thought maybe you might want sum't. Mrs. Penwarden said she wanted firewood, an' we're going out tomorrer for a load of the best."

The old man set down his plane and produced a clay pipe. Dick Lake picked up a shaving and chewed it. The impression Bony received was that those present were to debate in solemn conclave the subject of firewood.

"Don't want ironbark," said Penwarden. "Too hot. Burns out the stoves and the fireplaces. Where you going?"

"Over t'other side of Sweet Fairy Ann," replied Moss. "Fred Ayling's camped down by Watson's Creek. Sent in word that he's cut a hundred tons of mixed—chiefly box."

"Oh! And how much of a load you aim to get back with over Sweet Fairy Ann?" demanded the carpenter.

"We always take our full issue," interposed Dick Lake. "Ten ton."

"You won't be bringing no ten tons over Sweet Fairy Ann."

"Who says so?" asked Moss.

"I do," replied Penwarden. "The track won't take it. Your truck'll slide down off it and end up in the river."

"D'you think?" Dick Lake grinned at Bony. "I c'n drive that there truck to hell and back without scorchin' her."

"Twenty-two bullocks, a table-top wagon, and two men slid off that track in '15," said the old man. "And afore they all reached the river the slope of Sweet Fairy Ann broke loose and went down after 'em. You ain't been over that track."

"Twice," asserted Dick Lake. "Since the last time, Fred Ayling's shored her up a bit. She'll take our loading all right."

"What'll you have—pine or Oregon?" offered Penwarden.

"How much?" Moss drawled.

"Do the Oregon for twelve pound apiece," answered the old man.

"Watertight and all?"

The blue eyes flashed.

"All my coffins is watertight. Better order now for one apiece— if you will go for to try to bring a ten-ton load out over Sweet Fairy Ann."

"We'll bring 'er. How many tons you want?"

"The ten—if you get 'em out."

Lake got up from squatting on his heels.

"Okey doke," he said, and then turned to Bony, adding:

"Like a trip? See the country . . . and some."

"Be leaving at seven sharp in the morning, and get home about five," supplemented Way.

The good cheer accompanying the invitation captured Bony. Old Penwarden stood with a match burning to the pipe halted before his mouth. Bony nodded acceptance. The two men moved toward the door, and the shorter said:

"Pick you up at the pub sharp at seven. Bring your lunch, but no beer."

"Why no beer?" Bony queried.

"You'll see . . . tomorrer."

To Bony, Penwarden said between puffs at his pipe:

"Do you one in Victorian blackwood, Mr. Rawlings, sir. Twenty-five pounds, and guaranteed to fit you like a feather mattress."

REBOUNDING INFLUENCES

A full week, and the little gained wasn't worth writing to Superintendent Bolt.

Bony had explored the locality both on foot and in Bolt's car. Regularly before each meal he had appeared in the bar and had drunk too much beer. Forced by his pay and responsibilities to keep a tight rein on his generosity, he met with no necessity to squander money, as these people were too sturdily independent. There were some, like Lake and Moss Way, who accepted him; others were more reserved, chiefly, he guessed, because they wouldn't risk being drawn to the spending level of the pastoralist.

The Washfolds he found reticent about themselves and unhesitant to talk of others, but as they had been here only three years, they were in the same category as himself.

Behind this life at the hotel was another which was an influence on the general community rather than of it. Strangely enough, old Edward Penwarden appeared to be the representative of the inner life, this ever-present influence behind the community at Split Point.

By inference rather than reference did Bony learn from the old man of this section of the community. It would seem that it had withdrawn itself before the march of intruders who had bought land and built holiday homes, had withdrawn itself into its own country behind the inlet.

There were the Wessexes, Eli and his wife, their son who had gone to America after the war, and their daughter who had suffered mental illness following the death of her lover. There were Tom Owen and his wife, a childless pair, and Fred Lake and his wife who had borne fourteen children. There were two other families who, also, had been here for generations. And as far as Bony knew, these people seldom called at the hotel for a chat and a drink.

Excepting Dick Lake.

He was an ordinary, easygoing Australian to whom life is a game to be played always with a smile no matter what the jolts. You meet this type in the Interior, and it is these men who have brought all the honour to the country's arms in war. Nothing daunts them, nothing makes them winge, and within them are forces which only extraordinary circumstances ever bring into action.

The incident of what appeared to be an attempt to suicide seemed to have no bearing on the murder at the lighthouse. Bony was still not certain that the girl had intended to suicide. He had memorised her footprints made with low-heeled shoes, and although he had not again come across them, he had seen again the prints made by the man who had knocked her out and dragged her from the cliff. That man was Dick Lake.

At that scene, or shortly after, was the man Tom Owen, who had denied seeing either the girl or Lake and, later, had joined Bony on the dark road and pressed for information, at the same time urging the attractions of Lorne as against those of Split Point.

From conversations with Penwarden, there was no doubt that the girl was Mary Wessex, and that that afternoon was not the first time she had evaded her watchful mother. It was understandable that Lake would hurry her home, and that Owen would deny having seen her, for Bony, the witness, was an intruder from whom must be kept family skeletons.

That Dick Lake had been employed as a casual labourer with the Repair Gang was a fact not contained in the Official Summary. Fisher had been asked when he had inspected the lighthouse. He had been asked what men comprised the Repair Gang, and he had given the names of those men employed permanently by his department. To Fisher, a casual hand was not an employee of the department, and, consequently, he hadn't bothered to enlarge his replies to take in what to him was of no importance.

During those weeks as a casual hand, Lake could have made impressions of the lighthouse keys. He certainly knew of the work of constructing the locker in the wall. He knew as much as the foreman of that gang, but could be suspected of murder no more than any permanent member of it. All Bony had so far achieved was possibilities.

As was his custom after dinner, he donned an overcoat and set out for a tramp. The evening was quiet and the sea was lazy, and one couldn't foretell from what point one would next hear the surf. Above the distant lights of Lorne a new moon lay on her back like a wanton, and down by the creek of the inlet the frogs voiced the same idea.

Bony took to the inlet road, passing first several summer houses, then an opaque square from which issued the noise of an accordion, and which he knew was a tent occupied by the builders. He passed the home of old Penwarden and his wife, and outside this house stood a utility. The front door was open and voices drifted out to him. He passed the closed building where caskets plain and jewelled were created by an artist. Onward from this point the world was dark and vaguely vast beneath the brilliant stars.

It wasn't much of a road—just a narrow track surfaced with gravel reflecting the starlight sufficiently for one to keep to it. For a mile it skirted the edge of the inlet bowl on which were grazing sheep. At a gate to a paddock he halted to lean against it, and now that the sound of his footsteps had ceased, he could hear many undertones of life and the muttering of the distant surf.

He was reasonably sure at the end of this first week that the murderer he sought was a member of this local community. The killer was familiar with the interior of the lighthouse and kept himself up to date with its inspections and renovations. With all these local people the lighthouse was a dominant influence. Every boy and girl on entering the age of adventure would want and would succeed in climbing those steps to see the light, to marvel at the sun valve, to watch the play of the jets within the encircling prisms. They would come to know as much about the light as the engineers.

Leaving the gate, he proceeded along the country road which soon afterwards divided at a junction, the road to the left leading to the farm occupied by the Owens, and that straight ahead leading to the farm at which lived Eli Wessex and his wife and daughter. Bony kept straight on, walking smartly and enjoying the warmth of the exercise.

Crime is like the impact of a stone on placid waters. The stone had been dropped in this locality ten weeks before this night, and Bony was confident that the waves it produced were still expanding and contracting as influences in human minds. Mental influences produce physical action, and Bony was waiting to note an action that he might follow the influence causing it to its source—the dropped stone.

On seeing a light among the trees ahead, he experienced astonishment that he had walked four miles from the hotel, for the light was within the house occupied by the Wessex family. From daytime exploration, he knew he was within a few yards of the road gate beyond which stood the house within its fenced garden.

A dog was barking, and he was sure the animal was not alarmed by his approach but wanted freedom from the chain.

On arriving at the gate, he decided to go no farther. It was then that he heard the approach of a vehicle far back along the road, and the noise emerged slowly from the nearer throbbing of a small-powered petrol engine running the electric-lighting plant. It was several minutes before he decided that the motor vehicle was coming his way, and another passed before he saw its headlights weaving among the trees.

To avoid being recognised and thereby raising suspicion, he moved to stand against the trunk of an ironbark.

The engine was left running when the driver got down to open the gate. He had to pass into the beam of the lights, and then Bony saw Tom Owen. The man drove the vehicle to the garden gate, leaving the road gate open, and Bony recognised the utility which had been standing outside old Penwarden's house.

A second chained dog added its barking to the first. A veranda light was switched on, and the truck's lights were turned off. Bony could plainly see Owen walk through the garden gateway to the house veranda steps, where he was welcomed by a woman. She was tall, and her hair was light grey and drawn to a "bun" at the nape of her neck.

What they said, the barking of the dogs prevented from being heard. The woman went inside and was followed by Owen. The veranda light was turned off, but the front door was not closed. Bony waited—for no tangible reason. The stars said it was a few minutes after eight.

The barking of the dogs dwindled to desultory complaint. In the tree branches above Bony a kookaburra throatily guffawed like a satisfied devil pleasantly dreaming. Then the silence pressed down upon the invisible earth until a sepulchral voice moaned:

"Ma . . . poke! Ma . . . poke! Ma . . . poke!"

It was restful standing there against the excessively rough bark of the tree, only the watchful mopoke aware of him. This was Bony's world, where Time meant nothing and the lives of even the grandest men of no more moment than the nuptial flight of the termites. Bony felt no curiosity in Owen's visit to the Wessexes. These people were good neighbours.

Four miles! Four miles back to the hotel, and a leaping log fire and a drink before bed. Bony had actually left the tree when the veranda light sprang up and he returned to the ironbark to wait till the truck's lights would not reveal him.

Tom Owen appeared. He was followed by the woman Bony was sure was Mrs. Wessex, and after her came a younger man whom Bony thought to be the hired hand, Dick Lake's brother. The three left the veranda and approached the utility. The dogs again broke into excited barking.

The lights of the truck being extinguished, the three persons were indistinguishable when they stopped at the rear of the vehicle. The tailboard fell with a clang to the extremity of its supporting chains, and then Bony could just make out that something was being taken from the truck—a heavy object requiring both men and the woman to lift. Burdened thus, they moved towards the garden gate, where they were careful to negotiate the narrow entrance.

Now the veranda light held them, to reveal Tom Owen proceeding first and taking the weight of the forepart of the object, with the youth taking the other end and determinedly assisted by Mrs. Wessex.

Along the short path they staggered and lurched to the veranda steps, where Owen managed to turn without losing his grip and proceed backward up the steps.

What Bony thought they carried drew him from the tree, in through the gateway, to the very fence encircling the house. The carriers lifted their load to the veranda and immediately beneath the light. The object gleamed redly as slowly, slowly, it was taken into the house.

It was a coffin, the casket in which Bony had been invited to lie that Penwarden might be assured it would take comfortably the body of Mrs. Tom Owen.

A MAN AND A DOG

At eleven Bony retired to his room, his programme for the next day altered by the message left by Dick Lake that the trip over Sweet Fairy Ann "was off." At eleven-fifteen he turned out the light and sat on the side of the bed, wearing his overcoat and hat and his pockets weighted. At eleven-thirty he opened and closed the bedroom door without noise, and as silently closed the front door after him as he stepped out to the veranda.

Stug shifted himself off the door mat just in time to escape being stepped on. It was so dark that Bony couldn't see him, and thereafter he knew the dog accompanied him only by the occasional touch of a cold nose to a hand.

Man and dog crossed the lawn, climbed through a fence, walked down the slope of an open paddock, and so gained the highway without nearing the road lights.

Ten minutes later they reached the gate in the tall iron fence surrounding the lighthouse, and here Bony squatted on his heels and fondled the dog. Even thus he couldn't distinguish the animal, but knew by its behaviour that they had not been followed.

Under the snarl of the everlasting surf the night here was as quiet as it had been at the gateway to the Wessex homestead. Above man and dog the light pierced the sky with faint lightning flashes —four within the period of twelve seconds, followed by the eclipse.

"As we cannot hear anything suspicious, Stug, we must begin work," he murmured, and the old dog softly whined his pleasure in his voice. "I am going to leave you outside the gate and hope, I expect vainly, that should the gentleman who tiptoes about lighthouse yards come this way, you will warn me. You know him, of course. You recognised him when he entered the yard yesterday, and I bet he made a fuss of you, and you pranced about him. I know because you were panting when I came out of the lighthouse. He was a small man, and he came and went away on his toes when there was no real necessity. You think matters over and then tell me who he is, what he's like to look at. If you don't, I'll tell you, perhaps."

Stug objected to being shut out, and Bony heard him scratching at the bottom of the gate and ordered him to be quiet. It was, of course, the safest hour to make this visit without being observed. And the safest time of the year, too. Back on March first, there were people living in the lightkeepers' houses, and in those on the slope behind them. Then the weather was warm, and the sea enticed. It did happen, however, that late in the afternoon of March first it began to rain, and continued steadily until after midnight. The rain would have kept people indoors.

In the beam of his flashlight the banks of gas cylinders looked like rows of medieval armour. For a moment he stood directing the beam on the bottom step of the spiral stairs, and when he switched off the torch a light gleamed on the metal steps, went out and again gleamed, as though someone higher directed his torch downward. It was the indirect reflection of the light passing down the stair well, and Bony decided it was possible to mount to the light by the aid of those distant automatic flashes. It was also possible for a man to watch another ascending the steps and shoot him.

56

Down here, however, the light was too weak to enable him to locate the case on which he had sat talking to Fisher. He found it pushed behind the bottom step and placed it before a small heap of refuse swept against the wall. Seated on the case, with the torch to assist him, he proceeded to delve into that heap.

There wasn't much of it, and he knew what he wanted. There were scraps of oily waste, a short strip of oiled paper, fibrous material used for packing joints, and wood shavings. There should have been dust and other material, but it had been swept together by the investigating detectives, and they had removed all items likely to provide a clue.

Bony recalled the litter of wood shavings in Penwarden's workshop and remembered also seeing among this rubbish a shaving similar in colour to those which sprang from the coffinmaker's plane. He found the shaving of red wood among those of Victorian hardwood, a mere inch and a fraction wide, the width of the board from which it came indisputable.

He compared it with shavings taken from Penwarden's workshop. The grain appeared to be identical. The colours seemed to match, but only daylight could make him sure on this point.

He found no other shavings of red gum among the many in the refuse. There was nothing else of any value—Bolt's men had seen to that—and no one would have attached value to the solitary red-gum shaving save the man who had spent what doubtless Bony's superiors would term an idle hour at a coffinmaker's bench.

He had himself flicked a wood shaving from a trouser cuff, following a call on old Penwarden. If the shaving found here was identical with the red-gum shavings in the workshop, it must have been attached to someone's clothing and been thus conveyed to the lighthouse.

Whose clothes? If through elimination it could be proved that not one of the investigators and not one of the Repair Gang had entered the workshop, it would be reasonable to assume that either the victim or the murderer had been inside Penwarden's workshop on or before the night of February second.

Moving the case so that he could sit with his back to the wall and face the bottom steps, Bony rolled and slowly smoked a cigarette.

It was utterly silent. With the door shut not even the sound of the pounding sea could intrude. He smiled at the thought of hearing Stug giving a warning of the tiptoeing gent, and this thought sent him to the door with a short splinter of wood from the refuse.

The door could not be locked from within. As it did not swing freely, nothing save man-force would open it. He was tempted to withdraw the key, but as this might arouse suspicion in the mind of anyone interested in him, he ignored the key and set the splinter of wood against the door. Should anyone open that door whilst he was up top, he would at least know of it.

Back again on his case to finish his cigarette, he pondered the possibility that this investigation was at last about to break before the implacable assault of patience. Did the wood shaving found here prove that either the victim or the murderer had brought it from Penwarden's workshop, then the old man knew him. And as the old man had failed to identify the victim, then the shaving must have been brought by the murderer. Thus Penwarden knew the murderer, but not necessarily that he was a murderer.

Bony began to mount the steps, and the noise of his shoes on the latticed steel was like the falling of small hammers on an anvil. He tried to move more softly, and found that no matter how softly he trod, his feet made a noise which appeared to fly upward and race about the top floor like the feet of small children. The steps offered no litter which might have been overlooked. He passed the first of four little slot windows in the massive wall, and was careful not to direct his torch through it.

Coming to the first landing, he paused with a foot on the first of the next series of steps and pictured the murderer standing there like that. A little farther up was the locker in the wall, and it was opposite the locker that the victim's prints had been found on the stair rail. He recalled that the post-mortem had indicated that the killer was higher than the victim when the fatal shot was fired.

He went on up to halt at the locker. As at his previous visit in the daytime, so now was he assured that the door to the locker could not be noticed by anyone ignorant of it. At night, with his own torch turned off, the reflected flashes from above revealed neither its shape nor outlines against the wall. The murderer must have known the situation of this locker.

He recalled an assumption with which he agreed. The body weighed eleven stone, or one hundred fifty-four pounds, or something like one and a half hundredweight. That would be about thirty pounds less than a three-bushel bag of wheat. For the purpose of deduction, the weight of a filled wheat sack would approximate the weight of the dead body.

During the midsummer months, at every rail siding in the wheat-growing areas, men carry filled wheat bags from truck to stack, often trotting up narrow planks to the higher elevation of the growing stack. They do it all day long—men who have acquired the knack in the use of shoulder and neck muscles.

From the bottom of the step on which he stood at this locker there were forty steps, and any toughened wheat lumper could carry a hundred-and-eighty-pound bag of wheat up these steps. The bag would be hard and unyielding, and would be balanced on the man's shoulders.

Carrying a body up these steps would be an entirely different tax on human strength. The body would be yielding. A toughened wheat lumper could carry up a dead man and arrive "blown out." A lesser man could not accomplish it.

Assuming the murderer to be merely the average man, and unaccustomed to wheat lumping, it would be easy for him to drag the body down the steps and lift and push it into the locker. The foundation of the assumption that the murder had been committed on the steps, or at the top, was firmly laid.

Yet the cement of the foundation for this assumption was not expertly mixed. The murder could have been committed outside the lighthouse, and the body brought to the picnic ground by car or truck. Although it was raining, it was not cold that night, and people sleep with windows open on summer nights. Someone would certainly have heard a car or truck going to and returning from the lighthouse itself.

Bony was inclined to think that the crime had been committed by two or more men who had brought the body in a vehicle to the picnic ground and then carried it. That certainly indicated intention to place the body in the locker, intention based on the knowledge that it would remain there undiscovered at shortest for two months.

Bony decided to erase from his mind the temporary inhabitants and concentrate on the permanent residents.

Arriving at the upper floor, called the Light Room, he employed his torch to probe behind fixtures, and his hands where the torch could not probe. He found nothing. He did think of unbarring the door and passing outside to the balcony, but the thought was not one that lingered. Instead he mounted the steps to stand beside the light, a moth fascinated by the recurrent strokes of lightning, waiting in the dark of the eclipse for the brilliance to return.

Again in the Light Room, a flash illuminated his watch to tell him it was ten minutes after 4 A.M. He was astonished by the passage of hours, and dawdled no longer. His torch stabbed downward into the stair well, and as he descended, often he leaned over the railing to send the beam far down . . . to be sure no one waited. With relief, he passed the locker and, on reaching the lowest landing, needed to control the impulse to look back and up. Imaginative and actutely sensitive to strange surroundings, he had never conquered, despite varied experiences, fear of violence and of death.

Arrived at the door, he found the wood splinter as he had left it. Thrusting the door open, he sidled round the frame, just in case someone was waiting. But no one was there, and he locked the door and passed silently to the yard gate. He locked that and, pocketing the keys, became aware of Stug.

Stug bumped against his legs. An invisible tail flailed him. A hard object was crashed against his knee. He spoke softly to the dog and started off for the hotel. Then he became aware that the invisible dog was vigorously worrying something, growling and racing about with it. He told the animal to "drop it" and behave himself, and Stug banged his "find" against his ankle.

"All right!" he said, faintly exasperated. "Give it to me."

A shoe was thrust hard into his hands. Unable to see the dog, he knew it waited to rush away after the tossed shoe. He raised an arm to throw the shoe, desisted, brought his arm down and felt the shoe.

Beneath the dog's saliva, it was quite dry. It was also quite new.

TREASURE-TROVE

It was one of Bony's axioms that Time is the investigator's greatest ally. Time, through his inherited gift of observation, provided him with the shaving which examination in daylight convinced him had come from the place where a wise ancient laboured lovingly to build coffins. Time, through friendship with a dog, provided him with a new shoe which was to prove to be the hammer with which the shell of this mystery was broken open.

The shoe was so new that the leather under the instep still retained its original gloss. It was a size seven and dark brown, and, basing his judgment on the price he had last paid for his shoes, Bony estimated the cost of this one, with its fellow, as about five guineas. The maker's name was stamped on the inside, a name renowned for quality.

Unfortunately, it was so new that the wear to the sole and heel could give nothing of the character of its owner.

Stug would not have found the shoe at great distance from the lighthouse yard. Superficially, it would seem that because the shoe was new it must have come from the inside of a house. On the slope down from the lighthouse were several houses, but at this time only one of them was occupied. As it was early winter and the nights cold, it wasn't likely that the occupiers of that house slept with the doors open. Had it been an old shoe . . . Old shoes are tossed out with the garbage.

The murder victim had worn size seven shoes.

There was no necessity to call the dog when Bony left the hotel shortly after ten the next morning and walked down the highway to the turnoff to the picnic ground. The sun was shining, and towards the ocean the wide bar of white sand shut in the creek and kept out the breakers.

As Bony mounted the headland slope the cliffs lay to his right, and to his left were the summer houses behind those once occupied by the keepers of the light. Now and then Bony softly cried "Sool-em, Stug!" and the dog ran about with nose to ground and tail vigorously flailing. Nothing much happened whilst they were on the slope, save that a rabbit broke from cover and Stug merely glared at it.

At the graves of the two pioneers, Bony halted, watching the dog, and Stug lay down for a rest. From the graves it was but a short distance to the lighthouse fence, and when they stood outside the locked gate the dog began to evince additional interest in this adventure.

He ran about with nose to ground and then returned to look expectantly at his companion. He remembered the incident of the shoe and that Bony had kept it from him. Bony walked on and skirted a house, whereupon Stug lost interest. No, the houses meant nothing to him. They returned to the yard, and again the dog remembered the shoe.

This time Bony proceeded towards the seaward cliff, and almost immediately Stug ran on ahead, nose to ground, following an old pad. On the pad were the dog's tracks made the previous night. The pad wound among the bushes of tea tree, finally emerged into the open but a few yards from the cliff and gave out. But Stug ran on to the cliff and disappeared over its edge.

When Bony stood where the dog had disappeared, the beach below was that section where he had buried the penguin and from which he had witnessed what then appeared to be attempted suicide. In fact, he was now standing where the struggle had occurred between the girl and the man. The drop was sheer to the sand below—sheer save for a narrow ledge which began at Bony's feet and slanted steeply down the face of the cliff.

The ledge passed from sight several yards to Bony's left, and beneath a distinct overhang. There was no sign of the dog who must have gone down that ledge—for dogs do not fly off into space. One could step from the cliff verge to the beginning of the ledge, did one have nerve enough to stand on a pathway nowhere wider than twelve inches, and often less. At its higher end grew tufts of grass, and brush sprouted from the cliff face. Lower down there was nothing save rocky protuberances an experienced alpine climber could use for handhold.

Suddenly the dog appeared coming up along the ledge. He appeared from under the bulge of the cliff, and he was exceedingly excited. The narrowness of the pathway worried him not at all. Clenched between his teeth was a shoe. Arrived at the top, he playfully snarled, dropped the shoe, and ran a short distance, where he waited for the shoe to be tossed.

Bony picked it up, vented a sigh of immense satisfaction, and, after effort, managed to push it deep into a side pocket. It was certainly the fellow of Stug's previous find which now was locked in Bony's suitcase. The dog was disappointed but not dismayed. He returned to the cliff and trotted down the ledge. A little way down he stopped and, managing successfully to turn about, he barked invitation to the man to follow.

Go down that ledge! Not for a million! Bony cried "Sool-em!" but Stug declined to sool anything if his cobber wasn't game to go with him.

That at least one brand-new shoe had been lying somewhere down that ledge was proven. Bony thought of assistance, of ropes. He considered the feasibility of being lowered below that overhang, and then imagined the rope frayed to breaking point. Down beneath the overhang might be other articles of clothing thrown over the cliff by the murderer he sought. For a split second he considered calling on the police at Lorne to assist in the investigation of the face of this cliff. The thought quickly expired, and before he was actually aware of it he had stepped from the verge down to the ledge.

Men perform great feats for small reward. There are many who play the game of life with the dice loaded against them. Bony turned to face the aged face of Split Point and proceeded to shuffle along the ledge. Slowly he sank down from the verge, and then he was beneath the edge of the cliff and gripping weathered rock with both hands. His mind fought back Thought which was panic.

The dog turned again and ran on down under the overhang. He could be heard vociferously urging Bony to follow him, and Bony knew that to hesitate, to go back to safety on firm ground, and plenty of it, would achieve nothing but the acknowledgment of common sense. Provided the ledge didn't give under his weight,

63

provided he did not stop to look down, provided the rocky protuberances he chose to grip did not part from the cliff face, he would continue to live.

When the ledge took him under the overhang, he felt like a bristle under a giant's chin. The wind slapped the back of his clammy neck. The beach was an electromagnet increasing in power to drag him from the gold knobs of the vast golden wall. The sea hissed like serpents about his feet, the soles of which tingled with exquisite agony. His gripping hands were white like marble. And in his ears thundered the voice of pride:

"Go on, craven! What about the great D. I. Bonaparte now? Not so good, eh? Keep going—the dog's ahead of you."

The ledge rounded a curve. He could see it from the corner of his eye. It was now a little wider, sixteen to eighteen inches. He reached the curve at the narrow shoulder, passed round and saw, just beyond, Stug waiting for him, Stug standing on a tiny level area and barking encouragement, and behind Stug the small dark opening of a cave.

He must have held his breath all the way down, for when he stood on the little platform with Stug, his lungs panted for air. With his back to the cave entrance, he gazed out over the smiling sea, and all he could see was water. He could not see the beach, and realised that no one on the beach could see him—or the mouth of the cave. He looked upward, and nowhere could he see the top of the headland. There and then he decided that never, never would he walk back up that ledge.

Then he was conscious of the dog nuzzling the back of his legs, prodding him with his nose, growling and shaking hell out of something. Still panting, he turned about to see Stug with a man's waistcoat, and the dog backed into the cave, continuing to growl and worry the garment.

The entrance was a trifle less than five feet high and little more than three feet wide. Bony went in after the dog, and inside was able to stand upright. It appeared to be occupied.

That was the first impression Bony received. On the floor of rough rock lay a man's clothes, and with them a small suitcase. Memory of his ordeal was erased from his mind as he stooped to examine the clothes, ranging from a light raincoat to underclothes and socks, and when Stug interfered, he shouted angrily and then repented and petted.

"You lie quiet, Stug, and leave all this to me. I'll give you my own waistcoat to tear to pieces when we get out of this place. You lie down and take a nap. Just watch me smoking a consumption tube and trying to regain my habitual calm."

He sat down beside the clothes, and with trembling fingers managed to roll a cigarette and light it. With his head on his fore-paws the dog watched him, his great black eyes unwinking.

The suit was of good quality and in good condition. It was navy blue, and the colour and quality of the material and the cut more than hinted that its owner had been a seafaring man. The tailor's name had been cut from the lining of the coat. The coat buttons were of bone and gave nothing. There was nothing in the pockets save a wallet. There was nothing in the pockets of the trousers, but the buttons gave a clue, for they were of metal and on each was stamped the name of a tailor in Adelaide.

The wallet contained eight ten-pound treasury notes, a five-pound note, four pound notes, and seven shillings and fivepence in coins.

The raincoat was of poor quality. In the right-hand pocket was a wristlet watch and a gold signet ring. The watch was good but not expensive. The ring was broken. It had been broken previously and soldered. On the hexagonal plate were engraved the letters B.B. Like the suit coat, the raincoat had been deprived of the maker's tab.

"We can now, my dear old pal Stug, say that robbery wasn't the motive," Bony told the dog. "And can even assume that the murderer wasn't particularly intelligent. He removed the tailor's name from the suit coat and didn't notice that the trouser buttons bear the tailor's name. He was cautious enough to remove the maker's name from the raincoat, and that, I think, was unnecessary, because the raincoat is probably one of hundreds turned out by its maker."

The shirt and the tie were expensive, and the underclothes turned out by the mills in thousands. The socks gave nothing. The hat was of a popular make and sold to the retail trade by the ton. The victim's head size was Bony's size.

There was no doubt in Bony's mind that these clothes were once owned by the dead man found in the lighthouse. Although the floor of the cave was dry, the clothes were faintly mouldy and felt slightly damp, a condition to be expected of clothing exposed to sea air for several weeks.

"Leave that alone," he said to the dog, nosing into a much smaller cave at the base of the far wall. "What have you there?"

He crossed to see, and found a dead sheep.

The sheep had been dead for several days, and obviously it had starved to death. The dog winged, and Bony looked at him.

"So that's how it was, eh?" he said. "The poor sheep was feeding on the cliff top, and it came to the verge and saw the tufts of long grass growing on the ledge. It went down for the grass and then found it couldn't turn round like you do. So it came on down the ledge, and didn't have sense enough to go up again. It stood on the little platform and bleated for days. No one came to the beach below, to hear although not able to see it. And towards the end, Stug, the sheep came in here to die in the darkest place.

"You followed your nose to find out all about the smell. Nothing but the smell attracted you, because you're too well fed at home. And you found the shoes and remembered how, when you were a pup, you loved to pounce on shoes and sneak them out of the house and bite them to pieces."

Patting the dog, he returned to the clothes, was reminded that one shoe was still in his pocket. The shoe he removed and placed it with the wallet, the watch, and the ring. He removed buttons from the trousers and added them to the treasure-trove. In his mind was the unavoidable climb up the ledge. He cut the bottom from the leg of the trousers, preserving the cuff, inside which would be dust which the experts might make something of.

The clothes were then neatly folded and stacked on a rock shelf which the dog could not reach, and the suitcase examined. It contained a suit of cheap pyjamas, a hairbrush and comb, shaving out-fit, and a small brown paper parcel. The parcel contained thirty-three ropes of pearls. More than probable, they were imitations.

Two strings he pocketed, and the comb because it imprisoned hairs. The remaining articles he replaced, and put the case on the rock shelf.

This was not a cave known to visitors as those beach caves were known. It was not a place to be visited by anyone not driven by hard necessity. The murderer knew of this cave, and he had risked the journey down the cliff face to deposit here his victim's possessions. He must have used rope or straps to clamp the clothes and suitcase to his back, for he would certainly have had to use his hands to grip the rock.

Still swayed by the satisfaction given him by this discovery, Bony leaned his back against the wall of the cave and rolled another cigarette, and as he smoked his gaze wandered from the uneven floor to the dead sheep, from the sheep to the walls, the shelves, and the crevices. Hope was fleeting that there was another way to the cliff top.

Midway up the opposite wall he espied a niche. As it was large enough for a man to crawl into, and might lead to the top, he went over and felt within, as the shadow was heavy. At once his fingers touched metal, and in the next instant he knew the metal to be rusty keys. He ignited a match to look at them—two keys similar in size to the lighthouse keys. Dropping them into a pocket, he groped into the niche and brought out a thick wad of paper.

On his knees at the entrance to obtain full light, he saw that Time had pulped the paper but had not obliterated the evidence that once the wad had been magazines bound together with string. He managed to part the wad, to bare a page. The print was so blurred as to be unreadable. He tried again, and made out lines like an etching, and after study was able, with a little guesswork, to read: "Jack Harkaway's Adventures in Greece."

Back at the niche, he found a ball of twine so rotted he could barely handle it. There was a Y-shaped piece of wood with material fastened at the ends of the fork. Once it had been a boy's catapult. He found a book which, like the "Jack Harkaway Adventures," was pulped by time and the sea air. He could read nothing within the leather covers, but the spine bore the indented letters reading: "Cora. .s.and by R. M. Bal.an e."

Further groping brought to light a cigar box, and strangely enough, this box was well preserved. It contained foreign coins, a penknife, snapshots faded beyond determination, and sea shells. Finally drawn out was what proved to have been a box of matches, and four clay pipes which had never been smoked.

All this junk Bony put back in the niche, his mind fired by the knowledge that once this cave had been a boy's dream of coral islands and pirates bold. Only boys would have the nerve to negotiate that ledge now awaiting Napoleon Bonaparte.

The ledge! He would have to return via that ledge to life and eventual triumph. There was nothing more to be discovered here. He buttoned his coat, passed out to the level place before the cave, spoke to the dog, and faced the golden cliff.

The dog followed, sure-footed, supremely confident. A gull cried from somewhere in the glaring sky behind him. Go on, Bony! Don't stop! You are loaded with treasure-trove, the doubloons and the pieces of eight of success. Not so hard, is it? Better than coming down. The ledge took your weight coming down, it will take your weight going up.

Slowly he drew near to the top. Another foot or two would bring his eyes to the grassy verge of the headland. Better not look up. Be wise and keep the eyes busy locating rock knobs and crevices for handholds. A little farther, and he recognised a handhold he had taken when going down. He was at the top . . . almost.

The sky fell and the light waned. Pain shot downward to his feet, loosed his knees. The light continued to wane. Grip—grip! For heck's sake, grip! If the grip slips, there's only the beach below. Stop the light from fading out altogether. Will power might do it. If the light goes completely out, you'll certainly fall.

The light held, began to strengthen. Again he could see the cliff face, and his hands whitened by the strain. It was raining. The raindrops were sliding down his forehead, dripping from his nose. His legs wouldn't move . . . not at first . . . not till he shouted at them to move. The dog was barking from somewhere, perhaps the beach, perhaps the cliff top. It didn't matter. The surf was roaring like a vast herd of ravening tigers.

His feet and hands at last were moving. They had to move . . .

had to keep moving . . . Red rain was falling down his forehead, down his nose. He felt grass under his hands, and yielding sand touching his finger tips. He swam upon the grass, and then lay still with the toes of his shoes beating upon soft turf. An animal whimpered and a hot tongue caressed the nape of his neck.

BONY IS GENEROUS

Once upon a time Lorne was charmingly beautiful. Situated above a wide, sandy, and safe bathing beach, its doom was inevitable. Crowded hotels and a fun fair, souvenir shops and crude cafés attracted the flash elements from the city. When Bony saw Lorne, he shuddered.

Senior Constable Staley had become used to Lorne and the peculiar type of people who flock to it. He had always to be firm and natural. He was red, angular, abrupt. And he was ambitious. His "offsider," Constable Roberts, was his opposite, and therefore they made an excellent team.

Staley was writing a report when Roberts entered his office, lounged to the desk, wiped his nose on the back of his hand, and said conversationally:

"Bloke outside asking to see you."

"What's he want?" snapped Staley, without looking up.

"Just to look at you."

"Talk sense. Send him in."

". . . stated that on May 2, at about 4 A.M., he was outside the Hotel Terrific talking with a friend when a man came up to him and called him a ——," wrote Staley. He heard someone enter his office, and proceeded with his writing: "He did not know this man, and asked him what he meant by calling him a ——."

A gentle cough interrupted the flow, and Staley sighed, dropped his pen, and straightened in his chair.

"Well! What is it?" he barked at the slim, dark man seated on the only available chair. The dark man was lighting a cigarette, and over the burning match he said:

"I am Detective Inspector Bonaparte."

"And I'm——" He was about to add that he was Pontius Pilate when stopped by the warning in the brilliant blue eyes probing into his brain. "Yes, sir. I remember now, sir. A memo came to hand a couple of weeks ago notifying me you would be in the district."

"What is the condition of the road across the mountains to Colac?"

Now on his feet, Staley replied to the effect that the road was rough but passable. In reply to an enquiry about air services he said that Bony could catch a plane at Colac that night at eight for Mount Gambier, and at seven next morning a plane left for Adelaide.

"I could reach Colac by eight, I suppose?" pressed Bony.

"Yes, you could easily do that, sir."

"Then please make the plane reservation for me."

Staley reached for the telephone, and Bony cut in with:

"Firstly, however, contact a doctor and ask him to come here. I've bumped my head against a meteor or something, and it's rather painful."

Staley's light grey eyes became pinheads in his red face. Only now did he note that the caller's face was neither brown nor white but something like the colour of the dead ashes of a campfire. Crossing to the inner office door, he said stiffly:

"Constable Roberts! Bring Dr. Close. If he's out, telephone Dr. Tellford."

Dr. Close lived next door to the Police Station. He walked in three minutes later, and Staley introduced him. The doctor examined Bony's head, and Staley heard him ask what had happened and heard Bony say that a piece of rock must have fallen from the sky when he was out walking that morning. The doctor grunted, and Staley knew he thought this man's story didn't matter as he was in capable police hands. The doctor said that the blow must have been severe. However, the scalp did not need stitching and he would send in a salve to reduce the extensive bruising. And a slight sedative. When the doctor had gone, Staley said:

"Get that wallop through some funny business, sir?"

"I think it likely, Senior. I was on a tightrope when the rock fell on me. Be a Samaritan now and ask your constable to bring me a pot of tea and a couple of aspirin."

"Yes, sir. The sedative, though."

"I'll take that too."

Funny business meant personal violence. This Bonaparte had been seconded to investigate the killing at the Split Point Light-house, and that killing had been forward in Senior Constable Staley's mind. Split Point was in his district, and he had done his best in the resultant investigation. Again going to the door, he told Roberts to ask his wife to bring a pot of tea for Inspector Bonaparte. Roberts turned purple and hurried away.

A boy came with the salve, and Roberts took it in. When Mrs. Staley came to the back door with the tray, he took that in too, finding his superior engaged with the telephone and Bony rubbing the salve on sore places. He was passing out again when Staley snapped:

"Shut the door."

Staley was able to make the plane reservations, and then Bony was drinking his second cup of tea and looking more wholesome. On his desk had appeared a hair comb. From the comb his gaze rose to encounter the blue eyes.

"I want that comb to reach Superintendent Bolt," murmured Bony. "What would be the drill?"

"Post it to my Divisional Headquarters, sir, and they would send it to Melbourne."

"Far too much red tape, Staley. I hate red tape. And your Head-quarters would be curious. The Post Office might be faultless, but I cannot trust that comb to it."

"Roberts could take it to Superintendent Bolt if you gave the instruction. Has his own motor bike. He'd like the trip."

"Good! Let's pack it."

The comb was packed in cardboard and placed in a stout official envelope, Staley's curiosity mounting.

"Type a letter for me."

The uniformed man sat at the typewriter, and Bony dictated, following the usual procedure:

"'I am going to Adelaide for a few days. Meanwhile please have your people examine the hairs on this comb to ascertain if they came from the head of the man in the bath. I shall inform you when I expect to return to Lorne, and would like one of your senior men to be here when I do return!'"

Staley's grey eyes almost squinted as they watched Bony sign the letter and slip it into the envelope containing the comb. He had had to transfer from the detective branch to receive promotion to Senior Constable, and his ambition was to go back to the detective branch where he would be Senior Detective Staley. His gratification was keen when Bony said:

"Thank you for your co-operation, Senior. I shall not forget you in my final report. You could, of course, not know the contents of this envelope. It would be advisable for your Divisional Head-quarters to understand only that I asked you to have a letter de-livered to Superintendent Bolt."

Staley instantly agreed. He went out with Bony to the single-seater, saw him drive away to Colac, and returned to instruct his constable about the trip to Melbourne. If the hairs on that comb had come from the famous dead man, then . . . Who knows?

When, three days later, Staley was thinking of knocking off for lunch, Constable Roberts appeared at the office door, excitement in his dark eyes, his round face expressive.

"Car pulled up out front. Looks like the Chief Commissioner."

He vanished, and Staley swept litter into drawers and tidied his desk. He had just that period of time, when heavy footsteps sounded on the bare boards of the outer office.

The man who entered was moulded like a cigar. The top of his head, revealed when he hung his felt hat on a peg, was like pinkish marble rising from the fringe of greying hair resting on his large ears. Like his feet, his head was absurdly small in comparison with his waistline. It was known that his brown eyes could bore like a gimlet, exhibit infantile innocence, compel a sinner to shed tears of remorse.

"Good day, sir!" said Staley, stiffly erect.

"Day, Senior! Inspector Bonaparte not shown up yet?"

"No, sir."

"H'm! Said he would be here at one." The brown eyes bore into Staley, and Staley did not flinch by a flicker. Superintendent Bolt sat on the spare chair. "You heard from Inspector Bonaparte since he was here? Sit down."

"Thank you, sir. No. I've heard nothing from him."

Bolt produced a pipe and filled it from a tin of cut tobacco. Staley thought that superintendents should possess at least a tobacco pouch, if they would smoke a pipe instead of cigars.

"You know what he sent me?" Bolt asked, and Staley nodded, aware that prevarication would be useless. "Hair from that comb identical with the hair on the corpse in your lighthouse. Didn't tell you where he found the comb, did he?"

"No. He'd received a heavy blow on his head. Had a doctor see to it before he went to Colac."

"Bashed, eh! Not so good, Staley. Your Divisional Officer know about that?"

"No, sir. Inspector Bonaparte did not make a complaint . . . officially. Hinted that he wanted to by-pass D.H."

The large man grinned, slowly nodded his small head, regarding Staley as though he were a specimen bloodstain.

"I'll remember that," Bolt said. "Ballarat District could do with another senior plain-clothes man. Attractive?"

"Very much, sir. Job here is slow . . . drunks chiefly. Wouldn't——"

The door was opened and Bony stood smiling at them. Bolt heaved himself from the chair. Staley stood. He was faintly astonished by the look of relief on Bolt's face.

"Oh, Super! Nice of you to come down. Glad to see you," Bony exclaimed, and to Staley: "That road to Colac is disgraceful. I suggest we have lunch somewhere and gossip about the neighbours. Know a place where we can gossip in seclusion, Super?"

Staley had a brain wave. He said he was sure his wife would provide lunch if they would not demand sole Marnier. Bolt said he was dieting, and Bony voted for tea and a sandwich. It was Bony who insisted that Staley sit with them at the light lunch tastefully served by the Senior's wife. After lunch they sat in the small lounge, where Mrs. Staley assured them they could smoke to "their heart's content." And there Bolt glared at Bony and softly whispered the one word:

"Give."

"Those hairs came from the dead man's head?"

"They did."

"Then the clothes and the suitcase I found did belong to him. Actually, Super, I have had no doubt of it. Do we talk off the record?"

"Yes, yes," agreed Bolt resignedly.

"And our pact of non-interference is to continue?"

"Yes—blast you!"

"How like you are, Super, to my own Chief Commissioner," drawled Bony. "Well, to begin. Having decided I would have to locate the dead man's clothes—as your men failed to do—I found them, complete from hat to shoes. The suit was tailored by a small Adelaide firm who specialises in uniforms for merchant marine officers. It was built for a customer by the name of Baker. This Baker walked in one day, had himself measured, chose the cloth, paid for the suit, said he would return for it three months later.

"That was eighteen months ago. All that the tailor remembers about him is that he came off one of the ships and was a youngish man. On being shown a picture of your man in the tank, he thought there was a shade of resemblance—to use his own words. The cost of the suit was twenty-three pounds, and the books showed that it was paid for with cash.

"The underclothes and the shoes, having been manufactured by firms whose products sell all over Australia, give us nothing. The shoes are so new that I cannot assess the man's character and characteristics.

"Robbery was not the motive. There was a wallet containing eighty-nine pounds in notes and seven shillings and fivepence in coins. I now hand this money to you, Super. The notes and the wallet give nothing. The Adelaide people tried to raise prints. One singular aspect concerning the money is the coins found inside the wallet. Normally they would be carried in a trousers pocket. I incline to the thought that the killer pushed the coins into the wallet when he divested the corpse of its clothes."

74

Two poker-face men regarded the wallet Bony put down on a near-by chair. To the wallet was added a watch.

"When the murderer decided to hide the clothes to prevent identification, he removed that watch from the dead man's wrist. It also has been examined, without result. Jewellers and wholesalers inform me that the watch is not of a make or brand known to be on sale in Australia. The movements were made in Switzerland, and the case made in the United States, from which country it could have been exported to a jewellery firm in either Singapore or Hong Kong.

"Inside the case is stamped a maker's serial number which will enable you to trace the watch. There is, too, a number very faintly scratched, and my jeweller friends think it was done by a firm who repaired the watch at some time. I am informed that it is the usual practice of watch repairers to maintain a card-index system in which is recorded data covering the customer's name and address, when a watch is received and when delivered or posted to the customer. You might have enquiries made of all the jewellers and watch menders in Australia, excepting South Australia which has already been covered."

Bony paused to light a cigarette. Neither Bolt nor Staley spoke.

"With the watch, which was thrust into the pocket of the dead man's light raincoat, I found a ring, a signet ring." Two pairs of keen eyes looked at the ring set down beside the watch and the wallet. "You will observe that the ring has been soldered and is now broken.

"The jewellers to whom I submitted the ring did not rave about its value. In fact, they were professionally horrified to observe that although the ring is of eighteen-carat gold the solder used is nine-carat. They assured me that no goldsmith worth his salt would make such an error. They also assured me that even though the solder had come apart it had been applied by a man knowing something of goldwork.

"Find, therefore, the jeweller who has an apprentice or young assistant to do such work, and you may find the record of the transaction either in his books or in his mind. Thus the ring and the watch may give you more about this man calling himself Baker.

"You will see that the ring is engraved with the letters B.B., and doubtless the letters stand for Benjamin, Bertrand, or Bernard Baker. As the ring is of standard make and sold by the thousands, only the mistake made by the goldsmith will benefit our investigation.

"With the clothes was a suitcase, and inside the case was a brown paper parcel. Inside the parcel were thirty-three ropes of pearls. Here are two of them. They are imitation, and the retail price in this country is about five guineas."

The pearls were placed beside the other exhibits. Bolt waited for two seconds before asking:

"Where are the other thirty-one strings?"

Staley's interest was transferred from the pearls to Bony's face, on which was a beaming smile. He flashed a glance to the big man and saw there an expression of hope, fading. That an inspector should smile so at a superintendent astounded him and outraged his sense of discipline. What Bolt said shocked him.

"Won't give, eh, you little cuss. Not ready yet to give, and won't until you can say who killed our corpse—like Sherlock Holmes. Blast you, Bony!"

"But I don't know," protested Bony.

"But you know where you found the clothes and the suitcase. Where?"

"Where the clouds have a silver lining," Bony replied. "Now accept what I have given. Your dead man was an officer on a merchant ship. His name is Baker. He smuggles ashore imitation pearls on which to make a large profit. Surely, Super, with your great team of scientific experts you will quickly establish the identity of your corpse, his movements and associates. You have the watch repairs to help. And there is the ring. Let me have the information, and I will the more quickly tell you who killed him. Now make a note."

Bolt sighed as though with indigestion, and looked at Staley. Staley produced a notebook and pencil.

"I want to know whether any of your men at any time visited Mr. Edward Penwarden at his workshop. I want to know if any of the Repair Gang who worked at the lighthouse before last

Christmas ever went inside Penwarden's workshop. And if the foreman of that gang remembers having sent the casual hand to Penwarden's workshop for any purpose."

Staley completed his scribbling. Bolt said:

"Casual hand! What casual hand?"

For the second time Bony blandly smiled.

"Didn't know about the casual hand, did you, Super? Thought not. No mention of him in the Summary. No notice taken of the casual hand. Not important. No wonder you cannot obtain results."

Bolt's breathing was asthmatic.

"By crikey——" he began, and was waved to silence.

"No ire, Super, no ire. Bony must have his little triumph now and then. Now I must be off. Give my thanks to your wife, Senior. I'll call someday and thank her in person. Au revoir, Super. Don't follow me too closely, as I have to be careful of the company I keep. Let me know through Staley what is learned from those clues."

Superintendent Bolt had that look in his eyes which made sinners repent.

"You take care of yourself," he snarled. "I don't want trouble with your people, damn you. So long!"

He glared at Staley as both listened to the light footsteps crossing to the outer door. He sat down and, taking up his cold pipe, applied a match. Staley sat, too, and typed Bony's notes. Nothing was said as Staley boxed the clues safely, and when Bolt rose to go to his car he stared hard at Staley, saying:

"No dogging, now. That feller's as touchy as a young gal. But have business to do frequently at Split Point. We don't interfere, understand. You do nothing except keep a careful eye on his personal safety. And if he takes you into his confidence, you're lucky."

Staley stood stiffly. "Very well, sir." He heard the ponderous feet crossing the outer office, and when all was silent he said aloud:

"Am I coming, or am I going?"

THE PRODIGAL RETURNS

Other than its appearance there was nothing wrong with Superintendent Bolt's private car. In the boot Bony had found an old hat, a pair of rubber-soled shoes, a mass of fishing lines and spare hooks here and there, and it did not require effort to picture the Chief of the C.I.B. on vacation. A few miles on from Lorne, Bony drove off the road into a nook amid trees and promptly fell asleep, and was still sleeping when the sleek Department car swept the Superintendent by on his way to Melbourne.

At five o'clock Bolt's private car was again plodding along the Ocean Road, pounding up the rises and humming down the slopes, taking the curves with marked cautiousness. Bony was able to see the sea, and the gulls, to appreciate the beauties of this coast, but he sighed for the day when he might walk into a car salesroom and drive out a modern Buick.

Outside the bar of the Inlet Hotel stood two trucks and a car. He drove past these vehicles and parked the "plodder" in the open-fronted shed, removed his suitcase, and proceeded towards the front entrance, accompanied by a joyful Stug. He was, however, not permitted to avoid his friends. From the bar door issued Dick Lake.

"Good day-ee! How's it for a deep noser?"

The grin so slow to arrive was well cemented. Moss Way shouted that Mrs. Washfold said that the drinks were set up.

How could a man be an abstainer under those circumstances?

Moss Way relieved Bony of his suitcase, and Dick Lake grasped him by the arm and escorted him to the bar. The bar appeared to be full, and the large Mrs. Washfold was smiling and comfortably spread behind the counter.

"Welcome back, Mr. Rawlings!" she exclaimed. "Had a good trip?"

"Yes indeed," replied Bony. "Anticipating the temptations I would encounter on my return, I have been good. And now"—he lifted the glass of beer presented by Dick Lake—"and now here's to 'e all, and fill 'em up again."

"Where you been?" a voice asked, and Bony saw Tom Owen. The man's small grey eyes were faintly hostile, but no one detected hostility in his voice.

"Went through Lorne to Colac and on to Mount Gambier. Then north to Murray Bridge, over to Adelaide, and back again." Bony spoke lightly, and no differently when he added: "You can have Lorne."

"The place stinks," someone agreed, and Bony asked Moss if they had taken the trip over Sweet Fairy Ann.

"No! Been waitin' for you to go with us. We done a bit of work, ain't we, Dick?"

"Coupler loads from Dirty Gully and a trip to Geelong with old Penwarden's coffins."

"An' loafed around here drinkin' beer," added the licensee's wife.

"Go easy!' pleaded Way. "Why, we dug a coupler tons of spuds for Ma Wessex, and took 'em to Geelong with the coffins."

"Oughta packed 'em in the coffins," Lake supplemented. He smiled happily at everyone.

"Do you people export anything else besides potatoes and coffins?" Bony inquired.

"Yair. Wool and . . ."

"Empty beer casks," prompted a builder. Following the chuckles, someone said:

"Your missus gone to Geelong with Mrs. Wessex, Tom?"

"Went this mornin'. Should be getting back now. Reminds me."

Owen hastily emptied his glass and manœuvred a passage through the crush to reach the door.

"Plenty of time," Lake laughingly said. "They won't be back till late."

Owen kept going, saying nothing. A silence fell in the bar.

"Can't understand Tom being afraid of his wife," remarked a builder. "She seems inoffensive enough to me."

"Wouldn't put him in the doghouse, anyway," Moss said drily. "Funny bloke, Owen."

"I'll say," added a man with a walrus moustache.

"Aw, I don't know," defended Lake. "Old Tom's all right. Don't do no one any harm. Hey, Moss, it's on again."

"I'm always payin'," grumbled his mate.

Mrs. Washfold filled the glasses from a jug and said:

"Those women ought to be gettin' back. I'm sure Mrs. Wessex wouldn't be late of a purpose, what with Mary being a bit troublesome lately and her poor husband as bad as he is. Mrs. Lance was telling me——"

"Getting no better?" asked the builder of Dick Lake.

"Nope. All screwed up, he is. Seen him on the veranda when me and Moss was diggin' the spuds."

"What a shame!" exclaimed Mrs. Washfold, looking to Bony for support. "He'll miss The Reverence calling there. Mrs. Wessex told me last month that she simply hadn't time to read to him or anything, what with the farm work and all. Wanted him to go and live with her sister in Melbun, but the old chap won't budge."

"A total invalid?" asked Bony.

"Pretty well. Been extra bad these last six months."

"Uster be a tiger for work, too," interrupted Dick Lake, swaying like an orchestra leader. "Best axeman I ever seen. Had a lot of learnin', too. When we was kids he'd have us down by the barn and read adventure stories. All us kids liked old Wessex. Too right! And Ma Wessex 'ud cook up things for us to take fishing." The grin vanished for the first time this afternoon. "Uster read his head off, and now he can't hold up a newspaper, and there ain't no one to read to him. Like a lost dog, he is now. Wanted us to talk to him on the veranda, but Ma Wessex was on our tails all the time, huntin' us back to the bloody spuds."

Mrs. Washfold completed a swift circle and banged a tin box on the counter.

Everyone laughed and, the grin again in evidence, Dick hastily produced a shilling and dropped it into the box. Mrs. Washfold replaced it on the shelf.

"How's she comin' along this year?" asked walrus moustache.

"No faster for any help you give it," retorted the woman. "You boys don't swear as well as the visitors. We got to beat last year's effort. Poorest along the coast, it was."

"Forty-seven quid, wasn't it, last year?" said Moss Way.

"And six and tuppence. Bert found two pennies on the floor."

"Where does it go to?" Bony wanted to know.

"Children's Hospital. Over twenty thousand quid the hospital got last year out of the swear boxes," replied Dick. "Feel like havin' a go?"

"Be damned if I do," Bony said, and was instantly presented with the box. He paid the fine and the box was returned. To Dick he said: "You were talking about the bloody spuds."

They shouted as he paid another shilling, and Mrs. Washfold was happier than had the money gone into her till. She told the story of three anglers who deliberately cussed each other till each had contributed a pound.

Time passed and the men tended to break into small groups. Bony prevented this by insisting on again calling for drinks all round. He was beginning to feel the effect of the beer, and pretended he was far worse than he was. Clutching Dick by the arm, he said:

"How much does old Penwarden charge for those coffins?"

"Ten quid. Them he sends to Melbun."

"More for that one I saw in his storeroom, I suppose?"

"Too right. Beaut, isn't she?"

"Must take him a long time to bring up that surface on the wood."

"Months," said Dick, swaying towards Bony as though bowing to an audience. "Wipes an' rubs off and on for months. Waste of time on anything to be buried, ain't it? Old bloke won't make them redwoods for anyone, you know. Gets the wood down from the Murray."

"So he told me. Said that one in his store was for Mrs. Owen."

"That's right! Tom Owen took her home last week. Cripes! They can have it for mine. Blanket 'ud do me. Hullo, more playmates!"

The crunch of wheels on gravel vied with the purring of an engine. A door banged. Within the bar the voices sank to a low hum.

Two women entered, breasting the bar like men, to stand beside Bony, who happened to be nearest the door.

"Got back safe!" exclaimed Mrs. Washfold. "Had a good day?"

The younger woman giggled.

"Tired out. Evening, everyone!" She found Bony regarding her, his brows raised interrogatively, a ten-shilling note proffered to Mrs. Washfold. "Thanks! Just a tiny weeny one."

The men went on talking. Bony appeared to be entranced by the labels on the bottles back of the bar. The women chose gin and bitters, and Mrs. Washfold chatted with them about the price of clothes. Presently she said:

"This is Mr. Rawlings, who's staying for a week or two. Mr. Rawlings is down from the Riverina on a buck's holiday. Mrs. Owen and Mrs. Wessex."

Bony bowed. Mrs. Owen giggled, and Mrs. Wessex stared her interest. What these women had in common evaded Bony, for Mrs. Owen was small and birdlike and Mrs. Wessex gaunt and intense. Besides being older than Mrs. Owen, she betrayed unusual hardship and something of suffering. Labour had bowed her back, and the weather had etched her face.

"I like my holiday when and where it's quiet," Bony told them. "And I couldn't have come to a better place. I hope Split Point never becomes like Lorne."

"It will one day, I'm afraid," said the gaunt woman, her dark eyes probing.

"Then I hope not in my time . . . having only just discovered it." Mrs. Washfold butted in.

"I was telling Mr. Rawlings how poorly Mr. Wessex is these days. Might be an idea for him to take a walk out your way one afternoon for a talk with your husband. Cheer him up, maybe."

"I would be glad to do so," Bony took her up, and Mrs. Wessex said:

"From the Riverina! Are you a sheepman?"

"In a small way, yes."

Again her effort to assess him. Well over fifty, she was dressed sombrely in a fashion of twenty years ago. Nodding as though with approval, she said:

"I'm sure my husband would be glad to see you, Mr. Rawlings. One afternoon, perhaps. I shall be about the place somewhere. If

82

I'm not, go into the house if my husband isn't on the veranda. Ready, Edith? We must get along."

Mrs. Owen giggled at the company, and the men politely bade them good-bye. After their car had left, the atmosphere of restraint vanished. The licensee appeared.

"Those women will get home 'fore dark," he commented.

"Should do," agreed his wife. "Mr. Rawlings is going to visit Mr. Wessex. Have a talk to him."

"Added a shilling to the swear box, too," informed a builder.

"That's good." Washfold turned to his wife. "You clear out and tend the dinner, and I might kid these gents to put a bit more in."

Washfold "shouted" for everyone when his wife had gone. The conversation continued—clean—and Bony, feeling the growth of friendliness, was delighted by it.

Dick Lake's grin appeared now to be a fixture. Holding tightly to Bony's arm, he stuttered:

"Wash about that trip over Sweet Fairy Ann?"

"We dig spuds for Tom Owen tomorrer," interposed Moss Way.

"So we do. Some other day, eh? Great scenery, over Sweet Fairy. Y'know, Mr. Rawlings, you're good scout. Ain't he a good scout, Bert? Tell you what, Mr. Rawlings, if you wants a real good coffin to shove under your bed, I'll kid old Penwarden to make you one. Me and him is good cobbers. I'll see him about it tomorrow."

"We dig spuds for Tom Owen tomorrer," repeated Moss. "Come on. We've had enough."

Moss winked at Bony for support. Each took one of Dick's arms and resolutely moved to the doorway.

"One for the road," Lake laughingly demanded.

"We dig them spuds for Tom Owen tomorrer," repeated Moss.

"I won't dig no——"

Moss clamped a hand over Lake's mouth.

"We're not gonner pay no more shillings to swear boxes today," he said decisively, and with the assistance of Detective Inspector Bonaparte he urged the laughing Dick Lake to the heavy truck, lifted him into the cabin, and banged the door. Nodding cheerfully to Bony, he climbed up behind the wheel and departed with the horn going at continual blast.

ABOUT THOSE SHAVINGS!

Bony pushed at this Split Point mystery from all sides and heard never a creak.

Like the hidden root which defies the tree-pusher, there was a root of the local community hostile to his efforts to topple this murder mystery. He had decided that the sequence to the suicide attempt of Mary Wessex in his meeting with Tom Owen, and Owen's subsequent effort to induce him to go away to Lorne, was in keeping with the general reticence of conservative people. The incident of the person tiptoeing across the lighthouse yard when Fisher and he were inside was a hair of a different length, and would have had far greater importance in this investigation had Bony been sure that the blow to his head when on the ledge was delivered through human agency.

Only his will, energised by fear of falling to death, had saved him, and only the instinct of self-preservation had taken him to the grassy cliff top. There he had stayed for minutes before being able to sit up. He had looked for an assailant . . . he had examined the path and seen only the tracks of the dog and himself.

Bony remembered how the dog had stood by him and licked the nape of his neck, had barked and winged its concern, probably aroused by the smell of blood. Examination of the cliff edge immediately above the place on the ledge where he had stood when the blow fell quickly disclosed the bed of a fairly large stone. Near it was another stone which almost without effort he pushed into space.

In his search for proof, he sidled down the ledge to stop before those handgrips offered by the cliff, a protuberance of rock and a crevice. He saw that the top of his head was a bare twelve inches below the bed of the displaced stone, and thus could not be certain if he had been attacked or had been the victim of chance.

He searched the bare sandy places about the headland for a boot or shoe print size small seven or large six, the prints of the tiptoeing person, and failed to find such tracks, and when he had walked down the long slope to the sea to wash the head wound, the dog had evinced no sign of the intrusion of an unusual scent.

The Adelaide trip had given much ground for investigation but nothing conclusive. He had called on a detective friend of long standing, and had succeeded in gaining valuable unofficial co-operation. As the watch and the ring could not be linked with an Adelaide jeweller, and he felt his work was at Split Point rather than visiting every other capital city, he had had no reluctance to passing these clues to Bolt, knowing that Bolt would bring every State C.I.B. into the inquiry and pass the result, if any, to him. The Adelaide experts had found nothing of importance in the dust within the trouser cuffs, so this item had been kept from the Superintendent.

The day following his return was uneventful, and towards evening the bar was empty of customers save for one of the builders. This man and Bony were served by the licensee, and the conversation covered wide interests. The day had been dreary and wet, and gave no promise of the brilliantly clear day which was to follow.

Next morning, with Stug at his heels and the sun casting black shadows on the road, Bony went down to talk again with old Penwarden, in his mind linking the clue of the red-gum shaving he had found inside the lighthouse. To be greeted by the coffinmaker was to feel like the prodigal being welcomed by his father.

"Good day, Mr. Rawlings, sir. Come in and sit you down and chin-wag awhile."

"How are you today?"

"Oh, just the same. Sleep well and hearty, you know. You haven't been along lately."

"No. I took a trip to Mount Gambier. To look at the country. Better than mine. You're still busy, I see."

"I'm allus busy." The blue eyes twinkled. The scarred hands gripped the edge of the open sack being filled with shavings. "Old woman, you know. She keeps me up to it. If I've told you once, Penwarden, she says, I've told you a dozen times to bring me a bag of shavings."

"Useful to start fires, eh?" suggested Bony, drawing himself up backward to sit on the bench.

"The best thing out for starting a fire, Mr. Rawlings."

"An aromatic mixture, anyway. Red gum and Victorian hard-wood, with Queensland silky oak and a flake or two of pine."

"You're right."

The old man proceeded to fill his sack, and Bony kept the conversation to wood shavings.

"I assume that red-gum boards are harder to plane than, say, pine?" he remarked.

"Yes, a trifle. I likes workin' with pine, though. Likes to sniff the smell of pinewood. Clean kind of smell, pinewood has. Makes me think of the days I could go into the forest and fall and cut me own timber. Much pine up your way?"

"The natural pine, no. Good deal of it farther to the northwest of New South Wales. And that's no use for milling. Too small. Have you ever come across bloodwood?"

"No. Can't say I ever heard of it."

Attention to the shavings being rammed into the sack abruptly vanished, and the bright blue eyes in the fresh pink face expressed interest akin to that of the small child when promised a fairy tale.

"The most beautiful tree in the interior," Bony said. "Belongs to the eucalypt family. Comparatively rare, the best specimens are about thirty inches through a few feet from the ground. The sap runs the colour of blood, and the wood is the colour of blood."

The bag was left to fall and spill shavings, and old Penwarden came to the bench and sat on the sawhorse.

"Better'n Murray gum to last underground?" he asked.

"As to that, I can't answer. I do know that it's very slow-growing, and that the slower the growth of a tree the longer the wood will last."

"Aye, that's so, Mr. Rawlings, sir. My! I'd like a board or two of that bloodwood."

Having aroused keen interest in the subject of bloodwood, Bony passed to another, knowing that in the second subject the old man would be less mentally cautious.

"When are you going to start work on your next red-gum casket?"

The effort to follow into this second subject was visible in the old man's eyes.

"Well, that's tellin'. The one inside be took. Owen took her away last week." Penwarden chuckled. "I'm a bit lonesome without her. Don't like the place filled only with junk. A real red-gum coffin sort of makes the place feel respectable."

Bony smiled, and the old man waited for the joke.

"Was Mrs. Owen satisfied with it?"

Again the chuckle.

"Her husband said she was, but she wouldn't try her out like I wanted her to. You said that blood——"

"You'll have to begin work on another, just to keep in your hand and eye. When did you begin on that last one?"

"Begin on it! Oh, I don't rightly remember. Musta been six months ago, I suppose. Yes, all of that. Couldn't put me in a way of a bit of that bloodwood, could you?"

"Well, now . . . Y-es, I think perhaps I could. A great friend of mine lives in the top corner of New South. I might persuade him to send you down a log or two. You would have to have it milled."

Penwarden rested his hands on the knees of his drill trousers and beamed. The delighted smile completely banished the few wrinkles of age. They discussed ways and means of transporting a consignment of timber across hundreds of miles of virgin country to a Victorian railhead, and then to a milling firm just out of Geelong.

"I'd have to have a look at them logs before they cut 'em," Penwarden decided. "Can't trust no one these days to do anything right. Thank you very much, Mr. Rawlings, sir. You tell your friend to send me all the bill of costs."

"That will be fixed all right. There's one condition."

"What does she be?" asked the old man, abruptly anxious.

"That you let me know how the bloodwood turns out for your purpose. It'll be raw timber and you'll have to have it cured, and so you won't know for some time. But my friend and I will want to know what you think of it."

The smile flashed bright.

"Aye, of course I will, Mr. Rawlings. I'll tell 'e what I'll do. I'll make you and your friend a pair of book ends that'll reflect your eyelashes hair by hair. Aye, I'll do that for sure."

Then Penwarden wanted to hear of other woods which never came to market, and Bony described the Western Australian jamwood, which is the colour of and smells exactly like raspberry jam. He was extremely disappointed when told that the jamwood is a desert tree rarely large enough for commercial use.

Bony was hoist by his own petard. He became so interested and so caught up by the enthusiasm of this artist in wood that he failed to direct the conversation where he had intended, and rose giving promise to call again soon.

He had proceeded a full hundred yards along the road when he heard the old man shout and saw him beckoning to him to return.

"I'll tell 'e what, Mr. Rawlings, sir," Penwarden said, combing his long snow-white hair with his fingers. "There be no one now wantin' a first-class coffin, and, as you just told me, I must keep me hand in or go sort of stale on the junk. What about one for you, now? A good one to keep out the cold and wet for two or three hundred years? I've got the boards, and I could go right ahead."

Bony could only wonder at the blessing that such people lived to sweeten this age of raucous vulgarity. Trade certainly did not enter this proposition. He had advanced an offer to obtain bloodwood for no ulterior reason, because the offer was outside the planned conversation, and this humble man desired to counter his offer and so stand on equality. Slowly Bony nodded, and slowly he said:

"I think you are generous, Mr. Penwarden, and I thank you."

Again the cherubic smile, the eagerness illustrating so clearly the joy of the craftsman whose art is rarely appreciated.

"You come along soon, Mr. Rawlings, and we'll measure you for your first fit. Why, I declare, it's weeks since I did any proper polishing. It'll do me good. Meanwhile I'll look to the boards I has. Must be . . . let me see! I'm gettin' old all right. Yes, I remember. I began the polishing on that coffin for Mrs. Owen at the time they found that feller in the lighthouse. Constable Staley was here asking me about it as I was puttin' on the first coat. Now you come to-morrow for the first fit, and if you don't have no pallbearers, the shine on her will dazzle them that carry you into the cemetery."

With the music of Penwarden's chuckle in his ears, and in his mind too, Bony sauntered back to the Post Office, where he intended to despatch a telegram to that friend who thought more of his bloodwoods than he did of his bloodstock.

So Penwarden did not know that the coffin he had made for Mrs. Owen had gone into the house owned and occupied by Mr. Wessex. And Senior Constable Staley had entered the old man's workshop at the time of the murder and, on his clothes, could have conveyed a red-gum shaving to the lighthouse.

At three o'clock that afternoon Bony entered Staley's office. Staley stood.

"Day, sir!"

"Good afternoon, Senior. Sit down and let's talk. If you smoke, do so. No communication for me from Melbourne?"

"Nothing, sir." Staley relaxed—a fraction. From a drawer he produced a pipe.

"You have been here nine years, I understand, and you know the people at Split Point fairly well."

"Yes, sir, I think so."

"Know anyone there capable of bashing me on the head with a rock?"

"Plenty capable, sir, but the record of violence is clean. No out-and-outer like they have in Melbourne. That doesn't mean that there couldn't be, of course."

"Any people there named Baker?"

"Not that I know of," replied Staley. "There's a retired storekeeper of that name living here at Lorne. Family mostly married, and in Melbourne and Geelong. Superintendent Bolt said something about sending a man down to look into them."

"H'm! What d'you know of a man named Owen, at Split Point?" The red brows drew low to the small grey eyes.

"Nothing to his disadvantage, sir. Good citizen, by all accounts."

"Tell me what you do know."

Staley's information added little to that already gathered by Bony. Mrs. Owen was a sister to Mrs. Wessex, and it appeared that all the families behind the inlet were related. The Wessexes were the most well-to-do; the Lakes the least well off, but by no means poorly circumstanced.

"There are two young fellows over there named Lake and Way," Bony said, and again Staley's brows dropped.

"They're in partnership," Staley said. "Been together since young Dick came home from the Army. Way comes from Port Campbell, and of the two, I think he's the steadier. Hard-working, both of them. Dick Lake—he's the eldest son of that family—I understand he was a bit wild since he came back. Nothing vicious, mind you. Just careless about renewing his driver's licence, and forgetting to vote at elections, and very casual about cutting wood from the forest without paying the royalty. Merely the kind of thing which makes life hard for us country policemen. Nothing bad, sir."

"There's an Alfred Lake, isn't there?"

"Yes. Alfred Lake is Dick's next brother. Alfred works for Mrs. Wessex. I say for Mrs. Wessex because her husband is a chronic invalid. She runs the mixed farm with the help of Alfred Lake and her daughter. The daughter's a bit of a trial sometimes, I understand. But they're all sound people."

"There was, or is, a son, isn't there?"

"Yes, sir, I forgot to mention him because he's not on the scene. My predecessor—happens to be a pal of mine; we joined the Force at the same time—told me that Eldred Wessex was troublesome before he joined the Army in '39. No convictions, though. They say that after the war he went to America, and leaving Australia without coming home to see his folk made the old man bitter. Anyway, again according to gossip, Eldred Wessex is doing very well over in the States."

"And the girl?"

"Mary Wessex! She'd be about twenty-five or -six. Lost her man at the war. It upset her mind. Still, she's capable of looking after herself and is a help to her mother."

Bony fell to studying the wall calendar.

"Dense fog, isn't there?" he said. "I've been talking to old Edward Penwarden. Quite a character. What of him? His family?"

"As you say, sir, quite a character," agreed Staley, who was baffled by Bony's apparent lack of background, the absence of the undeniable stamp of the long-service policeman. "The Penwardens are highly respected. They've a married daughter in Sydney, and there's two sons. One is in the Customs, and the other in the Postal Department. Both about my age."

"You visited Penwarden at the time of the murder, so he says. Can you recall the date?"

Staley permitted himself to smile, saying:

"Yes, sir, I can. I was bawled out in court once, and ever since then I've kept notes on any case likely to put me in court." From a desk drawer he brought out a book and flipped over the leaves. "It was March third, at four-ten in the afternoon. Us uniformed men were working sort of independently of the plain-clothes team, and I called on old Penwarden on the off-chance he could give me a lead. Told me he'd seen the dead man and didn't know him. Couldn't remember having seen any suspicious character hanging around. Nothing else."

"Were you wearing uniform?"

The question astonished Staley, for it was a personal one. Stiffly he answered:

"As a matter of fact, sir, I was."

"Trousers, or breeches and leggings?"

"Breeches and leggings."

"Now tell me this, Staley, and I'll tell you the reason for these questions. Do you think it possible that when talking to Penwarden in his workshop a wood shaving could have become lodged between the bottom of a legging and the boot?"

"Possible, yes, sir, but unlikely. My leggings fit pretty well about my boots."

"Then tell me, after visiting Penwarden that afternoon, did you enter the lighthouse?"

Staley shook his head and referred to his diary.

"On leaving Penwarden, I came straight back to Lorne," he said.

Bony smiled and, having lit a cigarette, said:

"I am pleased to have that information, Senior, as I've been thinking that a little clue I have might be of no value. On the floor of Penwarden's workshop there lies a thick mass of wood shavings. A shaving from one of his red-gum boards I found in the lighthouse.

That shaving of red gum went into the lighthouse attached to some-one's clothes. Try to contact Superintendent Bolt."

Staley reached for the telephone, spoke to Exchange, replaced the instrument. Bony said:

"Sometime tomorrow, if you'll be co-operative, I want you to call on old Penwarden and find out if and when any plain-clothes man interviewed him in his workshop, and the name of the detective if Penwarden knows it. On February third and fourth the lighthouse inspector, name of Fisher, was working at Split Point. Ask Penwarden if Fisher called on him at that time. Shortly before Christmas last year, the Repair Gang was working at the lighthouse for five or six weeks. Find out if any of those men visited Penwarden at his workshop. Clear?"

Staley looked up from the rough notes he had made.

"Yes, sir. Where will you receive my report?"

"Probably come over here for it. Take long to get through to Head——"

The telephone smashed the quiet of the office. Then Bony heard Bolt's voice.

"I am interested in a heap of rubbish at the bottom of the steps," Bony said. "Composed chiefly of wood shavings. I want to know if the Repair Gang left those shavings or if Fisher left them, and the report, if any, of that rubbish made by your men. Clear?"

"Like soup, Bony," grumbled Bolt. "All right. Let you have it . . . where?"

"Care of Staley. Anything fresh your end?"

"Not yet. It's yours when anything fresh does come in. I give."

Bony chuckled. "So do I—when I'm ready. Cheerio, Super."

THE THREE BOYS

Bony was writing letters before the lounge fire when Dick Lake snaked in, still smiling. He was scrubbed and brushed and wearing his town suit protected by a navy-blue overcoat too long and un-buttoned.

"What about a shot of amber?" he asked.

Resignedly, Bony collected his writing materials, and Lake came forward to stand with his back to the fire.

"You seem determined to make me a soak, Dick. Are you going to a party?"

"Yair. To the pictures in Geelong. The mob's going. Fred Ayling came in this after, from his wood heap. Bit of a lad, Fred. You oughta meet him. Come on! Don't waste precious time. Gettin' on for six."

The small bar was filled to the door, and Washfold was working flat out. It wanted ten minutes to the fatal hour of six, and the enforced National Swill was in full flood. Above the general noise, rising like the blast from an atom bomb, was a particular voice.

"Fill 'em up, Bert. You're the slowest cow I ever struck. Hey! Who's driving that bloody truck? I'm not. I'm a gent for tonight. What! Another fine! What for? I never said nothing."

"Pay up! Pay up!" the company chorused.

"No more beer till you do," threatened Washfold, thrusting the swear box under the offender's nose. "A shillin' it is."

The offender was young. He was so square that the seams of his overcoat were dangerously taxed. His weathered complexion was as dark as Bony's, and in that walnut face the grey eyes held extraordinary vitality. He shouted on paying the fine, and he continued to shout because for weeks he had heard nothing but the wind in the treetops, the cries of the birds, and the clop-clop of his axe.

On Bony being presented, he offered an enormous hand which Bony wisely evaded. "You the bloke what was coming out to see me with Dick and Moss? Well, take it on. Sweet Fairy Ann will knock you. Won't she, Moss? Hey, Moss! Won't Sweet Fairy knock anybuddy?"

"You came over Sweet Fairy all right, anyway," someone pointed out.

"Me! Cripes, I'll drive a bl—— Ha-ha! Not this time. I'll drive a car or truck over any bl—any mountain in Australia. Shove that box outer sight, Bert."

Ayling badly needed a haircut. His face was chipped by the

recent application of a razor. He slapped a man on the back and almost broke his neck. Lake urged him to "go slow," and he pounded the counter with both fists and demanded a cigar.

"What is he like when properly inked?" Bony inquired of Moss Way, and Moss grinned and regarded Ayling with admiration.

"Quiet as Mary's lamb," was the surprising answer. "Ten beers and he goes to sleep."

Fred Ayling was standing squarely to the bar counter, and for a moment his hands rested on the bar, palms down. There was a splash of gold on the right hand, and the ring caught and held Bony's attention. It was a common signet ring. The engraved letters and the ring were identical with that found with the watch in the murder victim's raincoat.

Dick Lake urged his attention, but he was sure he had made no mistake when he turned to the smiling face so freshly scrubbed for the night out.

"Told you he was a character, didn't I?" Lake said, accent blurred. "Champeen axeman of the Western District last year. You oughter——"

"Time, gents!" yelled Washfold.

Someone outside sounded a truck horn, and kept it going. The din was shattering, and men poured from the small bar like the Keystone cops leaving a tiny van. Bony was swept with the tide, was vociferously urged to accompany the party, watched men swarm into and on a large truck, and waved them good cheer as they departed with Ayling's voice still dominant.

Nowhere in the Official Summary was Ayling's name mentioned, probably because the man was not at Split Point at the time of the murder. Later that evening Bony sat with the Washfolds before the blazing fire, and he mentioned Ayling.

"His pa took away his teethin' ring and give him an axe to bite on," Washfold asserted. "Clever feller, too, in his way. Get him on the quiet, and what he doesn't know about the birds and spiders and things would only fill an eggcup. Not much education, but a lot of knowledge."

"Been working about here long?" prompted Bony.

"All his life—exceptin' the war years. People had a farm back of the inlet, and they retired and went to live in Geelong. Fred joined up with the Navy when war broke out. Was on the *Perth* when she was sunk up about Java. Now he likes working on his own."

"Lonely existence, it would seem."

Washfold chuckled and looked slyly at his knitting wife.

"Peaceful, anyhow," he insinuated.

"Not natural, living alone like he does," objected Mrs. Washfold. "Speakin' to no one for months on end."

"He has the birds and the spiders and the ants to talk to. Could have a wife worse than the spiders," her husband murmured lazily.

Mrs. Washfold disdainfully snorted.

"It seems that he works in a very inaccessible place," Bony said. "Isn't there good firewood to be got much nearer to Split Point?"

"Yes and no, but that doesn't count with Fred Ayling."

"Mrs. Walsh said that he never was like other boys," interjected Mrs. Washfold. "Never took an interest in girls, but I did hear he was once very much in love with Mary Wessex."

"Might have done all right for himself if he'd had the education," supplemented her husband, and Bony adventured upon a question:

"Did you notice the ring he was wearing?"

"No. Anything out of the ordinary?"

"Nothing whatever. Merely that it looked odd for a man engaged in woodcutting, so far and for so long from civilisation, to be wearing a ring. He seems to be quite a hero to Dick Lake."

"Everyone speaks well of him."

Bony permitted the conversation to drift, and eventually told a little of himself and much of his sheep station. Washfold, whose knowledge of sheep and wool was extensive, was given no chance to fault him, and when the fire was permitted to die down they retired well satisfied with the evening.

After lunch the following day, Bony and Stug set out to visit Mr. Wessex, hoping to delve a little deeper into the background of the permanent residents, and confident that the invalid would be eager to talk.

The gulls were afloat upon the strip of creek within the inlet, and slowly approaching the zenith was a line of soft cloud, very high and almost rule straight. Despite the fact that the barometer at the hotel was high and steady, these signs denoted a rapid weather change likely to be violent. The sun was warming, and the air was still and redolent of marsh and sea.

Bony found Eli Wessex seated in a large invalid chair on the north veranda of the house. The dog who had been lying at his master's feet bounded to challenge Stug, but the invalid called and thus preserved the peace.

"Good afternoon, Mr. Wessex!"

"Good day!"

Pain had shrivelled the face, but the sunken eyes were keen. Pain had made ugly and useless the distorted hands lying on the invalid's lap. Eli Wessex was a shadow, but his mind was strong and virile. Nearing seventy, he looked ninety.

"Come along up and sit awhile," he said. "The wife told me you might call."

Bony mounted the four steps to the veranda and introduced himself.

"Fetch yourself a chair from the house," Wessex said. "The wife and daughter are out with the sheep. Me, I'm of no use. Just a hulk."

Bony brought a chair.

"But you are of use," he objected. "You cause me to be humble. As Joubert said: 'Think of the ills from which you are exempt. And thinking, be thankful.'"

The eyes lighted and the mouth firmed.

"There's wisdom in that, sir," Wessex said and smiled. The smile altered his face as sunlight alters the face of the sea. "Was it not Bishop Berkeley who said that a ray of wisdom may enlighten the universe and glow into remotest centuries? I hope you are enjoying your stay at Split Point."

"Very much so. The Washfolds are good hosts, and the people I've met are very friendly. You have a nice farm. Much better land than mine."

"All timber, big timber, when my father took up this land. He cleared most of it, and when I grew up I had to help him tackle the stumps. No wire tree-fallers those days. They had to be burned

96

and dug out and dragged away with horses. And once a year my father drove a wagon to Geelong to sell our bacon and cheese, and with the money buy necessities and cloth which my mother made into clothes."

"You were the only son?" suggested Bony.

"Two brothers and three sisters. The sisters are still living, and one brother. All did well."

"You have a daughter, Mrs. Washfold said."

"Mary, yes. A great help to her mother. We've a son, too. Doing very well in the States." The invalid gazed reflectively toward the tree-flanked slope of a distant hill. "Yes, Eldred's doing very well. We hope to see him again someday. Are you a family man?"

Bony spoke of his sons. Wessex listened with the intentness of one with whom exploration of another's mind was a rare pleasure, and later Bony sensed rather than observed bitterness behind the grey eyes. Whilst speaking of his youngest boy, little Ed who was no longer little, he wondered if the bitterness was occasioned by Eldred Wessex going to America after his discharge from the Army. Abruptly he changed the subject.

"I was invited to take a truck trip over Sweet Fairy Ann," he said. "Mr. Penwarden warned me against it, even warned Dick Lake and his mate that the track was too dangerous. What is your opinion?"

"Same as Penwarden's. Is Dick aiming to go over for wood?"

"Yes. Ten tons he intends to bring out."

"If I drove over that track, taking reasonable care, I'd end up in the river like the bullock team and wagon and driver did many years ago. Youth can get away with almost everything, and Dick is a youth who never had fear in him." The grey eyes gazed at the pure white cloud above the hill slope, and the tired voice went on: "Dick's father feared nothing—until a tree fell on him and smashed a leg. Dick's brother is another. He works for me. But he hasn't Dick's propensity for getting into trouble—and out of it. If you go with them over Sweet Fairy Ann, be sure to walk across The Slide. They won't be driving the truck faster than you can walk. Was Fred Ayling at the hotel last afternoon?"

Bony chuckled and described the reaction of human society on the lonely backwoodsman.

"Sound lad," Wessex said. "Always was. There were the three of them: my son and Dick Lake and Fred Ayling. Went to school together, the school right beside the hotel. It was closed a few years back, and the local children are taken by bus to Anglesea these days. Those boys rode ponies to school. They were good boys—real boys, you know—and a bit wild because we old folk who were brought up strictly tended to be slack in rearing our own children. It's the way of it—a kind of seesaw with the generations.

"My son, Eldred, learned too easily, had the gift of remembering. Dick Lake was a proper dunce, and he'll never do any good for himself. As for Fred Ayling—well, he was always a mixture. What he wanted to learn he learned without trouble, and what he wasn't interested in no amount of caning achieved results. When very small he began to study the birds and clouds and insects, and I used to tell him that if he would study such subjects as writing and reading, he would be able to put his outdoor studies to good use.

"But no. He can hardly put a letter together, and he can't spell the proper names of the birds and insects he knows so much about. Had it in him to make his mark in the world, but he's working alone in the mountains with axe and saw."

"Perhaps much happier than had he become a professor," suggested Bony.

"Perhaps. The unambitious are the happy folk. The younger generation think only of money. In their teens they want cars and want to travel. They want smart clothes and to ape their betters. Stay in the country and carry on when their fathers want to let go? No. Country life is no good to them. Let the old man die quickly. They want the cash. Never a thought to give in return. That's my son."

There were unshed tears in the grey eyes, and Bony concentrated on rolling a cigarette. He said:

"The Fred Aylings and the Dick Lakes are becoming a rare phenomena. Those three boys joined the services at the outbreak of war, I understand."

"They left home in the first month. Eldred and Dick joined the

Army. Fred went into the Navy. It was my fault, if it can be a fault. I used to read to them tales of the heroes who made England great and founded the British Empire. They had that in them, and each served his country well." Indignation crept into the voice. "I've nieces and nephews come to see us sometimes. They believe in nothing, and to them tradition is a bad smell. I can read their shallow minds. We've had our day. The world belongs to them, including what we laboured for."

The westering sun tinted the lined face with gold and whitened still more the close-cut hair. The golden shafts lay across Bony's shoulders. He was seated with his back to the veranda steps when the dogs barked and caused him to turn.

Coming from the barn was a girl, Stug and the other dog prancing beside her. She was walking on the tips of her shoes, and two fingers placed against her mouth unavailingly ordered the dogs to be quiet. On observing that she was noticed, she walked normally to the veranda, and Bony saw she was lean like her mother, and dark and vivid. Her eyes shone with lustre. They were almost blue-black. She was the girl he had seen struggling with Dick Lake on the cliff top.

She was wearing men's riding boots. As she came up the steps, her father said:

"What about a pot of tea, Mary? This is Mr. Rawlings come to visit."

Her only acknowledgment was a prolonged examination of the visitor which had nothing of either interest or welcome. Still regarding him, Bony was sure it was not to him she spoke:

"The dogs are home. Mother and Alfie can't be far away. It's raining over the jungle far away . . . far away. A pot of tea for Father and a man. All right . . . a pot of tea."

She passed on from the standing Bony and entered the house. In Bony's heart sprang profound pity, a flame swiftly extinguished by the sibilant warning seeping from unknown graves to him whose origin was partly chained to the spirit of their occupants.

The Evil Eye, Bony! Beware the Evil Eye!

Bony was directed to push the invalid's chair to the sitting room and place it beside the small table before the window. Books and newspapers on the table, the light from the window, and the position of the fireplace all indicated that here Eli Wessex spent most of his day when too cold or wet to sit on the veranda. The window view was of the approach to the house from the road, the small flower garden in the foreground, and it was not till several minutes later that Bony came to look at the room itself.

Flanking one side of the fireplace, bookshelves ranged from floor to ceiling, and few of these books were modern. Above the mantel was a picture of a woman seated with a man standing at her side—Mrs. Wessex and her husband when they were young. There were other pictures on the walls, and framed photographs upon the mantel either side the clock. The furniture was old, solid, valuable, well kept.

A pleasing room, and truly reflective of the character of those inhabiting it.

The voices of women came to them whilst Bony was trying to lift the depression weighing upon his host, and with a rustle of clothes Mrs. Wessex came in. She was wearing riding breeches and boots, and an old tweed jacket, and the wind had teased her hair.

"It was nice of you to come, Mr. Rawlings," she said, offering her hand. "Sorry I wasn't here. My husband, I hope, hasn't been grumbling too much."

"Thoroughly enjoyed getting it all off my chest," countered Wessex. "We've been talking of the rising generation, and of taxes, death, and damnation."

"What subjects! Mr. Rawlings must be bored—and thirsty. Mary's bringing the tea." She smiled at Bony and turned again to her husband, saying, with an edge to her voice: "The rising generation? What's wrong with the rising generation?"

"The same as our fathers thought of our generation," Bony said soothingly.

"Of course," Mrs. Wessex agreed, but her mouth had lost its softer lines. "The boys and girls today are no different from what we were. Not a bit."

"They are angels," said Wessex, and the bitterness was clear.

"Well, we won't talk about them," Mrs. Wessex decreed. "The afternoon's much too nice. Those ewes have lambed over a hundred per cent. Much better than last year. We left Alfie there to build a windbreak."

"H'm!" Wessex looked pleased but he wasn't going to sound so, and Bony learned that there were close to four hundred breeding ewes in a paddock two miles away. He was telling him that he owned twenty-two hundred breeding ewes, and that a lambing of eighty per cent was good in his part of the country, when Mary Wessex came in carrying a large tray.

The mother cleared the table and the daughter arranged the primrose tea set and the plates of scones and cakes. At this second meeting Mary never once glanced at Bony and, when seated beside her father, gazed beyond the window with a peculiar fixity of expression. The others talked of trifles, Bony thoroughly at ease, until the girl exclaimed:

"Car coming! Fred Ayling, like as not."

An old car halted at the road gate, and they watched the timber cutter crossing to the house. He moved with the litheness of a cat and the sureness of the horse, to enter the house as though he belonged, to stand in the doorway of the sitting room, his eyes alight, a smile on his weathered face. He was a trifle tipsy, but his voice was normal.

"Good-dayee, everyone! Just in time for a cuppa, eh? How's things, Pop?"

"'Bout the same, Fred."

"Come and sit down," urged Mrs. Wessex. "Another cup and saucer, Mary."

Ayling advanced, and the girl rose. The tautness of her face was gone, and she was smiling at him in a manner childishly pathetic.

"Day, Mary," he said, and patted her arm. "Bring a tough cup.

Might accidentally crush one of those in my fist. Not used to them sort. I didn't forget you."

Wessex was regarding him with open affection, his wife with narrowed eyes. The girl's voice was eager.

"What is it? You never forget—you never did." Swiftly she was serious, normal, and for the first time Bony saw her as she must have been before grief toppled her mind. "Sit down, Fred, and I'll fetch a cup for you. And some apple tart."

"Apple tart! That's the stuff, Mary. A large plate and full."

He sat between Mrs. Wessex and the invalid, smiled at them and at Bony, and Mrs. Wessex said:

"Going back to camp tonight?"

"No. Stoppin' at the Lakes'. Promised to on the way out."

"Did you enjoy the pictures?"

"Oh yes," was the reply—spoken, Bony thought, a little sheepishly.

"Tell me what they were about," suggested Mrs. Wessex, and Ayling laughingly confessed he had slept through the entire programme. When Mary appeared with the "tough" cup and saucer, he dived into a coat pocket and brought forth something wrapped in tissue paper. The flash of normalcy had passed, and the girl almost snatched the gift. He watched whilst she gazed at the package, obviously guessing the contents, and he chuckled softly when she unrolled the paper and revealed a marcasite peacock brooch. Fred Ayling reminded Bony of a good-tempered and playful bear.

Mrs. Wessex admired the brooch, and Mary had to jump up and stand before a wall mirror whilst pinning it to her dress. Bony felt sad at heart, for she was beautiful. For a little while she studied the effect of the gleaming stones and then turned swiftly to stand before Ayling.

"Was she young and buxom or old and bent?" she asked, and the question nonplussed him for a second. Then he said gravely:

"Old and bent. We encountered the *San Pedro* on her way from Panama to Cadiz. As the wind favoured us, she wasn't hard to take, and one of the voyagers was the old woman and her jewels the prize. I brought that diamond brooch home especially for you, my Bully Buccaneer."

Mary swept the hair back from her forehead, her eyes suddenly flaming.

"Ah! And there was much treasure, my Captain?"

"Gold by the chestful. But the diamond brooch was lovelier than all the gold."

The girl curtseyed low. Her father frowned. Her mother said stonily:

"That'll do. Come and drink your tea."

The girl laughed, and Ayling drew forward a chair. For a moment he was the reincarnation of Captain Kidd. Then once more he was the timber cutter in his go-to-town suit. Wessex coughed and looked at the mantel clock, and, saying nothing, his wife brought his tablets. He spoke of wool and, when Mary gave a low, chilling chuckle, determinedly continued to talk on the subject of wool. His wife sharply told the girl to clear the table.

Shortly afterward Ayling said he would have to get along, and Bony also rose to leave.

"Thank you for your hospitality," he said to Eli Wessex. "It has been a pleasant afternoon."

"Thank you for coming, Mr. Rawlings." The grey eyes pleaded. "If you could spare the time to call again? I can't shake you by the hand, but the wife will for me."

"I shall be glad to come again," Bony said. "Hope to be staying at the Inlet Hotel for another week or two. Good-bye, for now."

Mrs. Wessex accompanied the guests to the front veranda, and to Bony she said:

"Please come again. My husband would be awfully glad to see you." She called to Mary to hurry, and to Ayling explained that Mary was bringing "a little something for the camp." Ayling laughed and squeezed her arm.

"I know your little somethings for the camp. What's it this time? Half a side of beef?"

She patted the hand grasping her other arm. Her expression was unaltered, but her eyes were soft.

"Look after yourself, Fred, and don't take too many risks. And remember what I've told you so often. When you tire of being alone, come to us."

Mary appeared carrying a large and heavy parcel wrapped in newspaper. Ayling accepted the parcel and emphasised its weight by pretending to drop it. He chided Mrs. Wessex, laughed at Mary and lifted her chin.

"So long, all!" he said, following Bony down the steps. "See you again sometime. Be good!"

When Bony closed the road gate, both waved to mother and daughter. At the dilapidated car Ayling said warmly:

"Try and make it again, Mr. Rawlings. Old Eli's havin' a rough trot, and anyone callin' in for a chin-wag helps him along." He sat behind the wheel and deftly rolled a cigarette with hands as steady as those of a surgeon. "An' come out with Dick Lake and his partner to my camp. They'll be makin' it tomorrer. You'll be welcome for a billy of tea and a snack of whatever's in the parcel Mary brought."

"Thanks. I will. And I'll certainly call on Mr. Wessex again."

Bony nodded au revoir and departed. He heard the car engine roar, tone down as the vehicle was backed to take the track to the mountains. The noise of the engine died, and he glanced back. The machine was motionless, and Mary Wessex was standing beside the driver.

Bony walked on, happy because he felt he had given a little happiness to one whose ailment was tragic misfortune, and elevated by the company of people who gave with pleasure and received with humility.

In the face of his malady, Eli Wessex could easily be forgiven his garrulity. With all her problems, his wife could be forgiven her occasional sharpness of tongue. The daughter's mental condition was a separate tragedy, and the additional load placed upon her mother's shoulders was the absent son.

The one ray of sunshine in that home seemed to be Fred Ayling, a recluse, almost an eccentric. What had the old man said of Ayling? That he could have been someone today had he not been so unbalanced at school. That Eli Wessex and his wife both held Ayling in deep affection was certain. They had known him as a small child, racing to school with their own son and Dick Lake . . . with Mary trailing after them for sure.

Mary! What a pity! The years of waiting, of longing, and the thunderbolt striking from the New Guinea jungle. At one moment a haunted automaton; at another an excited child; for one fleeting moment a normal young woman. Bony recalled the scene when Ayling described the capture of the imaginary Spanish galleon.

Pirates and galleons and treasure! The girl had asked: "Was she young and buxom or old and bent?" For a moment Ayling had been puzzled, and then swiftly had understood. She was living in the past—must have been—when they two were playing at pirates. He had said he had brought the brooch especially for "my Bully Buccaneer," and she had called him "my Captain"!

Three boys and a girl playing pirates, fishing, riding, working at school together . . . the boys going off to war, the girl staying behind and waiting.

My Bully Buccaneer! Bully . . .

The ring on that finger so ably assisting other fingers to roll a cigarette was engraved with the letters B.B. The ring in the pocket of the murdered man's clothes also was engraved B.B. B.B. stood for Bully Buccaneers. That must be so.

The two rings were alike as two peas. Three boys and a girl . . . the Bully Buccaneers. The dead man in the lighthouse . . . the clothes in the cave . . . the ring in the coat pocket. The association of the ring with the nude body interned in the wall of the lighthouse could be assumed.

Three boys and a girl. The girl was Mary Wessex. One boy was Dick Lake, and another was Fred Ayling. The third was Eldred Wessex, who was said to have gone to America. Had Eldred gone to America? Was it possible that it was his body in the lighthouse?

It could be, but was it probable that there could succeed a conspiracy of silence over the identity of the body?

SWEET FAIRY ANN

The weather map showed the entire southern half of the continent to be controlled by an anticyclone, and the glass at the hotel registered 30.18 inches on the morning that Bony left on his trip over Sweet Fairy Ann. But the gulls were still loafing on the Inlet Creek, and another straight ribbon of high cloud was nearing the zenith.

When once off the highway, it was necessary to shout to make oneself heard above the clatter of the empty truck—no hardship to Dick Lake and his partner. Bony quickly gave up the effort. He was glad to be packed between the two men, who helped to cushion the jolts.

There was no one about the Wessex homestead, but smoke was rising from the kitchen chimney and several cows were placidly cud-chewing outside a milking shed. The farm gave way to trees which angled the track, and Moss had plenty to do with the steering wheel.

"Fred got this far, anyhow," remarked Dick Lake when they were crossing wet ground which betrayed the wheel marks.

"He called on Mr. and Mrs. Wessex yesterday afternoon," Bony shouted. "I was there at the time."

"How was he?" asked Moss.

"Just drunk enough to be booked."

"S'long as he didn't go on from Lake's homestead last night he'll be o.k."

"My ole man wouldn't let him go on last night," Dick said, and chortled. "Ruddy character. He's yellin' for more beer time we gets to Geelong, and we has a few at the Belmont, and then he sits down in the pictures, folds up and goes to sleep. And he don't wake no more till the pictures comes out. Then he wants crayfish for supper and we can't get only bacon and eggs, and so we runs around the town for two hours trying to find a fish joint open. Ends up with finding nothing open and has to come back hungry."

"Did well in the Navy, didn't he?" asked Bony when the truck was passing silently over a flat stretch of track. Dick chuckled and turned to present that most attractive grin.

"Shanghaied," he said. "There's me and Eldred Wessex and Fred goes up to Melbun to join the A.I.F. Been cobbers since kids and wanted to keep together in the Great Stoush. Gets to Melbun late that night, and next morning we agrees to meet outside Young and Jackson's pub at two, as Fred wants to see a sister what lives in Carlton.

"While he's waiting for me and Eldred to turn up at Young and Jackson's, Fred goes in for a 'quickie,' which he repeats until he gets to his sleeping stage, when he reckons we'd gone off to the recruitin' office without him. So he nabs a taxi and tells the driver to take him to the war office.

"When Fred wakes up, he's in the Navy recruitin' office, not the Army, and he's that dithered he can't tell the difference in the uniforms. So when he comes to, he's in the flamin' Navy what won't let him out to join me and Eldred what's in the Army."

"You two should have joined the Navy, too, and so kept with Fred," suggested Bony, and Dick explained the difficulty of thinking straight after searching two dozen hotels for a pal.

"Any'ow, it wasn't so bad," he said, yelling at the top of his voice and keeping himself down on the seat as the truck passed over a stony ridge. "That taxi driver could have taken Fred to the Police recruitin' office."

"He would have been properly sunk then," averred Moss. "More sunk than he was on the *Perth*."

The track flowed down to a depression between the hills and followed a stream about which grew tall white gums and ironbarks, with the ground so free of rubbish that the scene was not unlike a well-kept park. Travelling here was much easier, and more interesting, for Bony noted kookaburras and black cockatoos, kangaroos and trails of possums up the tree trunks.

An hour after leaving the hotel, the forest abruptly ended at a gate, beyond which was grassland divided by the track which merged with the dwellings of a distant farm homestead. As though halted by an ambush, when the truck stopped outside the main house it was immediately surrounded by shouting children of all ages, an enormous woman and a tall, crippled man adding their welcome to the din.

Mrs. Lake took charge of Bony, who noted two rangy youths lifting hauling gear and tackle to the truck, before being metaphorically carried into the large kitchen-living-room. The others trooped in soon afterwards, and all were regaled with "tough" cups of tea and huge mounds of buttered scones and buttery cakes, the butter being white and obviously homemade.

"Fred's about three hours ahead of you," roared Mr. Lake, as one long accustomed to roaring to make himself understood. The commotion was terrific. A lanky youth leaned against the wall. A small tot clawed at Bony's trouser leg and screamed to be taken up. A lath of a girl regarded him solemnly, and her mother's vast front shook as she tried to edge in an opinion or two. Outside, calves bellowed and dogs barked and the chooks crowed to vie with the shrieking of a caged cockatoo.

The rattle and creak of the truck was hospital-quiet by comparison.

Two of the youths now stood on the truck, maintaining hold by gripping the rear edge of the cabin. With them were numerous dogs which never ceased to yap excitedly, and though they had brought pandemonium with them, Moss and Dick shouted with unnecessary vigour. And about nothing. They were as two small boys taking a train ride to the zoo.

Like a sardine in the middle of the tin, Bony managed to roll a cigarette before they passed through the further boundary gate. He was thoroughly enjoying himself, and not far removed from the exuberant mood of his companions. The farm left behind, the forest closed upon them, and the track no longer so clearly defined as heretofore. Previously it had attempted a grade, had found an easy way among the hills; now it seemed to have taken leave of its senses and lost all caution.

Moss Way concentrated on his driving, and Dick Lake did remarkable feats with the wisp of cigarette which dangled from between his lips. The truck lurched and the engine roared and whined, and the back wheels bumped and sometimes felt as though springing off the ground. They were mounting a slope, following a trail left by Ayling's car.

They topped a ridge, but the trees were so massed that nothing could be seen of a vista, and then they were rolling down a deceptive slope, the truck in low gear to assist the brakes. Across a gully, splashing through water, and on and upward for hours, or so it seemed, and every yard the world limited by the forest of trees which blotted out compass points and often held the sun at bay.

"Old bitch's boilin'," remarked Dick.

"Yair. Not as good as she was," observed Moss. "Reckon she'll go to the top without seizing up?"

"Oughter."

The dogs were now quiet. The engine went through its repertoire, and constantly the driver shifted gears with lightning rapidity. Bony gripped the seat edge to keep his body down and his head from crashing against the roof, for the farther they proceeded the rougher the track.

Presently the trees thinned, became smaller. The sky with its sun began to take charge of the world, and swiftly dominated it. Then the trees gave out altogether and they were crawling just below a red-rock ridge, here like tessellated castles, there like a city of church spires. The trees became an arboreal floor, crumpled like a carpet after a party and littered with outcrops much like discarded orange peel. Only the crudest work had been done to make the trail sufficiently level to prevent a vehicle from toppling over, and how these men expected to bring back and down a load of ten tons was beyond Bony. It was hair-raising enough to be going up in the empty truck.

Eventually it seemed that the very sky itself stopped further progress, and they arrived at a little plateau where the truck stopped, the engine collapsed, and silence was a blow.

"There she is," Dick Lake said, opening his door and getting out. The dogs were already to ground to welcome him. The youths joined them, and Bony got down to stretch his arms and legs.

"Is this Sweet Fairy Ann?" he asked.

"Yair. Beaut, isn't she?" replied one of Dick's brothers. "Comin' up t'other side's worse, though."

"See a long way," said Moss, dragging a tin of water from the truck and proceeding to fill the radiator. "Not a drunk's track, this one."

"Why I said to bring no beer," supplemented Dick. "Even Fred wouldn't tackle this track with a drink in him, and if he tried to, my old man'd stop him."

"Where did the bullock wagon go down?" asked Bony, and was told it was farther on.

"We leavin' the tackle here?" inquired a youth.

"No, better take it down below The Slide."

Even the engine sounded refreshed by the rest, and again all aboard, the truck rolled across the plateau and gave Bony a shock. From the edge there was no track bar the corrugated rock, as steep as a house roof for a hundred feet or more to a ledge which curved from sight. The vehicle crept down the roof to the ledge and then hugged the rising wall of rock upon one side and shrank from the gulf on the other. Bony looked down. There was no bottom to the gulf save a faint white mist.

He wanted to get out and walk, but the wall prevented one door from being opened and there was nothing but space beyond the bottom of the other.

"Great view, ain't she?" obtruded Moss's voice. "That mountain over there we call Lightning Bill 'cos every thunderstorm coming across belts hell out of it. Wouldn't live there for all the tea in China. Hate lightning. Never could stand for it."

"Me too," supplemented Dick. "Them jungle storms put the wind up me."

The ledge slanted and curved about overhanging shoulders, reminding Bony of that miniature ledge leading down to the boy's pirate cave. He kept his gaze upon distant peaks, and the soles of his feet unpleasantly tingled. Lightning he thought preferable to heights, and to come out this way for ten tons of firewood appeared ridiculously uneconomical. He said cheerfully:

"I wonder if Mr. Penwarden has knocked up the coffins we ordered."

Moss laughed and Dick spat outside and chuckled. They were quite happy, and this made Bony inclined to annoyance. The ledge angled sharply, and he was positively sure that at the angle it was not wide enough to take the truck wheels.

Beyond the angle the gulf ended at a rock wall joining this with another mountain. Bony was greatly relieved until he saw that the wall was, indeed, just a wall and that beyond it the ledge went on to cross a precipitous slope of loose shingle.

"This is where the bullock wagon and all went down," remarked Dick. "Old Eli Wessex tells of it. He knew the driver and his off-sider. They never found 'em ... or the bullocks ... or the wagon. Got buried under the mullock what follored 'em down to the river."

"An' diddled old Penwarden outer his price for coffins," added Moss. "Looks like Fred's done a bit of patching up here and there."

The cut across the slope bore evidence of someone's labour with a shovel, and without hesitation, the driver permitted the truck to negotiate the cut. Bony expected the entire slope to give way, and again he wondered at the stupidity of coming over this mountain for a mere ten tons of firewood, which could so easily have been secured on the track back from Lake's farm, when he thought he had the answer. Fred Ayling lived in this vast wilderness, quite without reason save the one of living adventurously, and these friends of his were making the trip because it was hazardous and because it was beyond the mundane orbit of their lives.

Thinking thus, Bony felt relief when the truck crossed the slope and the ledge became a trail following an easier grade again to enter the forest. Half an hour, perhaps, and abruptly they came to a hut built of logs, with a bark roof, and a smaller shed roof over an open fireplace. The fire was blazing, and billies hung from a cross pole. Fred Ayling stood by the fire, and behind him pranced a pert Australian terrier.

"Good day, blokes!" he shouted.

"Good day-ee, Fred!" came the chorus, as the truck disgorged its human freight. "How's things?"

"Oke doke." Fred tossed fistfuls of tea into boiling water. "Better have it right now. Gonna rain soon and hard, and The Slide won't take too much weight." Grey eyes gleamed when they encountered Bony. "Day, Mr. Rawlings!"

One of the boys brought a tucker box, and another carried Bony's lunch basket, and everyone was invited into Fred Ayling's house. The house contained but one room floored with rubble from termite nests. The furniture was scant and fashioned with adze and axe, but so well built that Ed Penwarden would have been slow to condemn. For seats there were packing cases. Wall shelves bore the marks of the adze. They were laden with books, a camera, a microscope. Axes protected by leather sheaths and two rifles were suspended above the fireplace, and several framed photographs hung upon the walls. In addition to a fixed bunk there was a camp stretcher, the latter being in use.

Ayling brought in a large billy of tea and slammed it on the table to hurry the leaves to settle. Dick grinned with joy and his brothers evinced great respect for their host. The small terrier defied the visiting dogs and kept them outside.

"How d'you know it's going to rain?" Bony asked. "Not a cloud in the sky."

"Don't matter," replied Fred, filling tin pannikins. "Help yourselves to milk and sugar, gents. It's going to rain, and how! The spiders are flying."

"Grow'd wings, did they?" questioned Moss Way.

"Yair, this morning before I got home. Musta hatched yesterday, or the day before. Never seen 'em do that in winter. You blokes'd better load up quick and do a get, or you might be here for a fortnight or a month. Even the ants aren't liking it."

"What are they doin'? Carryin' their eggs around?" asked Dick.

"No, shiftin' the cows."

One of the boys laughed, respectfully, and Ayling explained.

"You see, when the spiders hatch, the first thing they do is look for something to eat. As there are thousands of 'em in a sort of flock, a lot of 'em get eaten. The rest climb to a height, such as a dead tree, and they wait for a wind to come. You know, a soft wind that you can hardly feel. When the wind comes, they let out a yard or two of gauzy silk which the wind carries upward with the baby hangin' to the end of it. The wind might take 'em for only a few yards, and it might carry 'em for miles. Where they come down is where they stop and grow up and mate and have a few million young'uns of their own."

They stood eating and drinking the hot tea.

"That right that the females always eat their men?" inquired Moss.

"They will if they get the chance, but sometimes they don't get it. Sometimes the old man's a bit cunnin'. I seen one old feller catch a fly, wrap him up nice and comfortable with web, and give that to the female to take the edge off her hunger. It's hunger what makes the female so fatal. I never seen it done, but in a book I've got the naturalist tells how the buck spider will rope his female's front legs so that after the mating she won't be able to catch him."

"Good idea. No woman's gonna catch me," vowed Dick.

"Don't like spiders," said Moss, and was supported by one of the lads.

"What's wrong with 'em?" questioned Ayling. "Spiders are man's greatest friend. If it wasn't for the spiders, man would never have survived the insects."

"Don't like 'em, anyhow," persisted Moss. "The bigger they are the less I like 'em. And them cows being shifted by the ants? Didn't know you had any cows."

Ayling laughed, and the others joined in.

"Go on," urged Moss. "I'll be the mug."

"Well, the ants keep aphis like we keep cows, and for the same reason. They look after 'em, and they milk 'em. They pasture 'em, and see to it that the weather don't catch 'em bending. I could show you if I had the time. But I haven't, and you're loadin' up and gettin' away snappy. Haven't got the tucker to feed all you coves for a month."

While this conversation had been proceeding, Bony was noting the more intimate details of Fred Ayling's abode, primarily to assess the man's character. The books on the crowded shelves were all protected with brown paper covers with no writing on the spines to indicate their subjects. There was an enlarged picture of an elderly couple, and in the man there was distinct likeness to Fred. There was another photographic enlargement of three young men in uniform—one a sailor and two soldiers.

"That's us," announced Dick Lake, observing Bony's interest. "Me and Fred and Eldred Wessex."

"Better get going instead of yapping," interrupted Ayling.

Bony stepped closer to the picture of three happy-go-lucky men so new to uniform they were still self-conscious of it. The second soldier, said to be Eldred Wessex, resembled in no degree either his father or his mother. The chin was weak, and the high forehead was too narrow. He had his sister's nose and the intensity of his sister's dark eyes, but nothing of the sweetness of her mouth and the firmness of her chin.

The others were leaving the cabin, and Bony went out after them. Moss Way tended the engine of the truck. The boys removed the ropes and tackle, and Dick Lake with Fred Ayling sauntered away among the trees. The sunlight was charged with gold and was warm . . . too warm and too golden. The birds were happy, or sounded so until one paused to listen intently for the subtle note of nervousness.

Bony went with those on the truck.

All about the camp were stacks of logs, each eight feet long and not less than fifteen inches through, each barked and without a particle of rot. Some had been split from logs of much greater girth, and here and there stood the stumps of trees having a circumference of many feet. An inescapable item of the scene was that nowhere had Fred Ayling's work resulted in devastation.

The men proceeded to load the truck, and Bony studied the manipulation of ropes and counterweights enabling Ayling to use a crosscut saw, and at another place he found a similar contrivance by which Ayling was able to haul his logs together into a stack.

A strange man to live here alone in the forest, to fell the giants by his own efforts and to deal with them by his ingenuity . . . and take time to study the insects and the birds. Happy to be a king without courtiers rather than a slave in the economic machine.

They loaded the logs and roped and twitched the load. They

climbed into the cabin and atop the load and drove away along the trail, the engine pulling in second gear, slow and steady. Arrived at the cut across the loose side of the mountain, the truck was stopped and all got to ground, save Dick and Ayling.

"Better walk," Moss told Bony.

Dick Lake proceeded to take the truck across The Slide. The others halted. Moss said:

"No reason for all of us to go down . . . if she gives."

"You mean that it's possible that track may give way?" asked Bony.

"Could do. Not likely, though, as Fred's had a good look at it," came the cheerful answer.

They watched the loaded truck crawling across The Slide . . . all for a load of wood . . . all for a social visit to a pal. It was preposterous, and Bony was aghast, for he was sure those about him were not braggarts. They began the crossing when the truck had reached the far side, and Bony glanced upward to appreciate the smooth slope and downward to see the same smooth slope of gravel extending to the edge of a tree belt hiding the river. How far down . . . it appeared to be a mile or more.

Beyond The Slide, Fred Ayling left the truck and turned back after cheery good-byes and a cool nod to Bony. The truck went on along the safer ledge, and as Bony, with the others, followed on foot, he wondered if imagination gave the impression that Fred Ayling today was a trifle less friendly. It appeared possible that he was displeased with Dick Lake for talking about the picture of the sailor and two soldiers.

The truck stopped, and when the walkers reached it the driver pointed to the western sky where the knife edge of a vast blue-black cloud mass was midway from southern horizon to zenith.

"Gonna come, all right," Dick said. "Must get past the old man's place 'fore she does."

They were halted at the foot of the rooflike slab of rock atop Sweet Fairy Ann, and the boys tossed down the rope and tackle. The tackle was fixed to the front of the truck and to a rocky projection, and Bony was offered a place with the team on the free end of the rope. The engine was revved and, in bottom gear, proceeded to force the truck up the incline—the crew on the rope running back, taking up the slack and giving just that added assistance to bring the vehicle to the summit.

Thereafter Bony rode in the cabin with Moss Way and Dick, who manhandled the steering wheel, and when they entered the forest again the sunshine seemed to turn green . . . until quite abruptly it vanished altogether.

The vehicle lurched and swayed, but the bumps and jars were absent. They managed to cross a wet patch by a fraction of effort from the driving wheels, and once were bogged and had again to employ the rope and tackle to get free. Dick answered Bony shortly. Moss said nothing, obviously anxious about the weather. The gaiety had left them, and Bony sought for a reasonable cause and failed to nail it.

Again they were welcomed by the Lakes and their numerous family. The dogs yelped and the calves bellowed and the children screamed. The Lakes were loath to let them go, and when they did there remained but little of the clear sky, and that a brilliant sea green.

"Looks like Fred's spiders knew something," Moss said. "Hope the rain keeps off till we pass Wessex' place. Didn't bring no chains, did we?"

"No," replied Dick

Further silence, which Bony broke.

"What made Fred Ayling take to the bush like that?"

"Just his way of it, I suppose," answered Moss. "Was in love with Mary Wessex, wasn't he, Dick?"

"Yair."

"But she wanted Phil Gough and he never came back from the war." Moss chewed his cigarette. "Life's funny, ain't it?"

"Bloody funny," agreed Dick, and Bony detected a snarl in his voice. "Why bring all that up? What's past is past."

Dick Lake's mood was as puzzling to Moss as it was to Bony, and he said chidingly:

"Oke doke, pal. You got plenty of spiders up your way, Mr. Rawlings?"

"Tarantulas, trap-doors and red-backs."

"Ants by the millions, I suppose."

"By the trillions," replied Bony. "Today has been just it to bring them all out. I was interested in Fred's story of the flying spiders, though. I've seen them drifting in the breeze."

"So've I. Ah, here she comes. Push her, Dick."

Dick "pushed her." Within a minute the rain bounced on the engine bonnet and reduced visibility to fifty yards. Three minutes later the driver had to handle a bad skid. Five minutes after that they reached the better road at the Wessex farm.

"Can be lucky," growled Moss.

The wind came, from the northwest, beating against the edge of the depression which had sprung from the Southern Ocean to confound the weathermen. One moment the rain was falling straight down, the next it was slanting to ricochet off the bonnet and smash against the windscreen.

"What's the time?" asked Moss, and Bony said twenty past five.

"Better go to the pub, Dick," suggested Moss.

"All right. We'll stop to get our coats. Walk back from the boozer."

Presently they came to Penwarden's workshop. The door was closed. A few yards farther on the truck was stopped and Moss cleared it to race through the storm to the camp for their coats. Bony said nothing, and apparently forced Lake to offer a comment.

"If this keeps up, the Ocean Road will be blocked at a dozen places between Anglesea and Lorne."

"Landslides?"

"Yair. Where the road cuts into the foot of the hills. Country round here is all loose. A drop or two of water makes it sludge."

The habitual grin was absent. The voice had lost its pleasing lilt. If Lake was in a raging temper he didn't show it, and Bony could recall no cause for his mood.

Moss charged back into the cabin, and they went on to stop outside the hotel bar, and so close that Bony merely had to step from the running board into the doorway.

The licensee leaned against his side of the bar, and as though to keep the counter in position, Senior Constable Staley leaned against the opposite side. No one else was present.

"Drunks and babies are blessed with luck," said Staley. "You fellers are extra specially blessed. You'll be taking The Slide once too often."

"Aw, she's all right," countered Lake. "What'a we having?"

"You got out in the nick of time, anyway," said Washfold. "'Nother half hour and you wouldn't have got to Eli's place. Full load, too."

"Did you go with them?" Staley asked Bony.

"Yes. Had a great day, in fact. Extraordinary country. And extra-good drivers."

"Can drive, all right. When sober." Staley grinned at the truck-men and called for drinks. He was at the end of the row, with Bony next him, and none saw him slip an envelope into Bony's side pocket. "How's your dad, Dick?"

"Pretty good, considerin'. Got a new brace for his leg what's much better than the other one. Was askin' about you."

There was no smile, no lilt in the voice. The policeman said he would fall for it.

"Pop hoped you'd go along and sample a new brand of cider he's got comin' to the boil. Wants you to pass out for a day or two while he markets a coupler thousand possum skins."

Staley chuckled, and Bony estimated the fine two thousand possum skins would bring to the lawbreaker.

"You haven't got those skins planted in your load, I suppose?" asked Staley. "You would go crook if I ordered you to shift all those logs right outside this pub."

"You're tellin' me," snorted Moss Way. "Shut up kiddin', Dick. Ain't we done enough work for one day?"

"Yair. Fill 'em up, Bert."

THE STORM'S CONTRIBUTION

The rain stung the iron roof of the Inlet Hotel, and the wind bayed about its eaves. Split Point was subject to the anger of the sea, and its embattled hatred of the land could be heard under the harsh dissonance of the nearer uproar.

Staley had departed for Lorne, and the wood carters had retired to their camp. The Washfolds were completing the day's chores, and Bony sat before the leaping fire in the bar lounge.

The sea air will at any time lay hot plates to the eyes of the visitor, but when the wind carries the spume inland for many miles, a pleasant lethargy becomes an irritation. Bony sat with his eyes closed and completely relaxed physically, his mind actively traversing the events of the day and the communications he had received from Senior Constable Staley.

The result of Staley's interview with Penwarden was definite. The old man said that no detective had entered his workshop, and that Superintendent Bolt himself had called at his house one evening and taken him in a police car to view the body which had been placed in the old school building. Bolt reported that no member of his team had visited Penwarden at the workshop.

The members of the Repair Gang, then in Melbourne, had been interviewed, and all had stated they had not visited Penwarden's workshop. They were indignant at the suggestion that the shavings examined with other litter and swept by the detectives against the wall on the lower floor had been left by them. Having completed their work, they had, in accordance with routine, swept clean the entire lighthouse.

At first Engineer Fisher denied making the litter, and then admitted that he had utilised part of his time in constructing a rocker for his small son. He had not swept out the litter, believing that no one would enter the lighthouse between then and his next inspection.

The litter, therefore, had been left by Fisher during his inspection carried out on February third and fourth, and thus the Repair Gang could be eliminated as the agent of the transference of the red-gum shaving from Penwarden's workshop. As Fisher stated that never at any of his visits to Split Point had he entered Penwarden's workshop, he, too, could be eliminated. There remained the victim, his murderer, and possibly the murderer's accomplice.

The ring brought nothing, but the watch had. A jeweller trading in Ryde, Sydney, had received the watch for repairs on January nineteenth, and had delivered the repaired watch to the customer, who called for it, on February sixteenth. The jeweller's records provided the customer's name as being Thomas Baker.

The jeweller failed to recognise his customer in the photographs of the body preserved in formalin. He agreed to the approximate age and general appearance of the man, and added that he thought he was from a ship. However, he was greatly helpful when he recalled that when the customer called for the watch he had been accompanied by a woman, and that during the transaction the woman had removed a glove and he had noted that her fingers were covered with rings set with opals.

Opal Jane! Opal Jane was a gentleman's friend. She was clever and respectable! She had more money in more banks than any "lady" in the Commonwealth. Yes, she knew Thomas Baker. What he did she didn't know, but "had the idea" he was a ship's officer. Yes, she had recognised Baker in the published pictures of the man in the formalin bath, but she had not come forward as she had no liking for "being mixed up with a murder."

Persistent interrogation failed to elicit further information from Opal Jane. She was "requested" not to leave Sydney.

Either the woman lied or actually believed that Baker's front name was Thomas. Were he the same man, and there was no reason to assume otherwise, he had given the initials B.B. when purchasing the suit of clothes from the Adelaide tailor . . . B. Baker. Bony found this oddity a little annoying, for a man will readily change his surname and rarely trouble to change his Christian name.

Although Bolt had reported nothing about the signet ring engraved with the letters B.B., Bony was confident that the hunt for the jeweller who had cut and soldered with a wrong solder would go on. There was certainly a thread passing from that ring to the dead man, as there was a strong thread from it to Fred Ayling. The thread passed through Ayling to Mary Wessex, who knew something of the Bully Buccaneers among whom were Dick Lake and Eldred Wessex.

Eldred Wessex! Everyone said that on receiving his discharge from the Army he had gone to America. Dereliction in filial duty had wounded his father—to the degree that no picture of him was in the living room at the homestead.

Were Opal Jane's statement accepted, the man found dead in the lighthouse could not be Eldred Wessex, the young soldier whose picture Bony had that day seen at Ayling's camp. The dead man's mouth and chin denoted tenacity; the chin and mouth of the soldier were weak. The dead man's forehead was broad; the soldier's forehead was narrow. No facial operation could create so wide a difference.

There was a plain thread between the cave in which the dead man's clothes were found, undoubtedly the imaginary headquarters of a juvenile gang of buccaneers, and Fred Ayling, who owned a similar ring to that found in the pocket of the raincoat.

Fred Ayling! There was a decided chain of reactions in which Ayling was an important link. Ayling had accepted him, Bony, the previous afternoon when, together, they had left the Wessex homestead. At parting, the woodcutter had warmly invited him to visit with Lake. Shortly after that parting, Mary Wessex had spoken to Ayling. On visiting Ayling with Lake, the former's demeanour was subtly changed. He had certainly not approved of Lake's action in drawing attention to the picture of the heroes three.

After lunch Ayling and Lake had walked to the first of the wood stacks, and together were in the truck when it was driven across The Slide. Prior to lunch Lake's attitude to him, Bony, had been cordial, but afterwards, when they were driving back to Split Point, Lake was surly to the extent of being noted by his partner.

The cause of the changed attitude in these two men must be in what Mary Wessex had said when she stood beside Ayling's car. Had she given a warning? She was sane enough to convey a warning acceptable to Ayling.

Mary Wessex! Mary Wessex was the person who had tiptoed across the lighthouse yard that afternoon Bony was inside with Fisher. Mary Wessex had tiptoed to the house from the barn when Bony was with her father, childishly enjoining the dogs to be silent. Her tracks left at the foot of the veranda steps were the same as those left in the lighthouse yard—when she was wearing the same boots.

It was reasonable to assume that Mary Wessex had seen him go down the ledge to the cave, and that she had waited for him to return . . . with a rock as a weapon to kill him. A man would have made sure, with a second blow. A determined and normal woman would have made sure too.

It was clear that the unbalanced Mary Wessex knew all about that cave. It was possible, even probable, that she knew nothing of the dead man's clothes deposited there, but were she a member of the Bully Buccaneers, she would place extravagant value on the secrecy of the cave to three boys and herself. To her he was a threat, a revenue officer, even the captain of a British frigate.

To Ayling, when told of his descent to the cave, he became a far greater threat, must have done, to change a sane man's attitude and influence the attitude of Dick Lake.

Ayling knew of the dead man's clothes and suitcase in the cave. So, too, did Dick Lake. Knowledge that he had visited the cave had made them wary of him.

Reviewing all this, Bony reached the opinion that when Mary Wessex apparently tried to throw herself off the cliff and was restrained by Dick Lake, actually she was about to step down to the ledge to visit the cave. Had Lake prevented her from doing so because he thought the descent too dangerous for her or because he could not permit her to discover the dead man's effects? How it happened that he arrived at the cliff in time to prevent her could not at this stage be answered.

The rings! There were, to Bony's knowledge, two identical rings. The letters B.B. more likely than not stood for Bully Buccaneers. Including the girl, there were four Bully Buccaneers, and it could be possible there were four identical rings. A jeweller might fail to recall using the wrong solder on one of them, but no jeweller would forget having sold four signet rings and engraving each with the same letters.

When the ring found in the dead man's coat was presented to Bolt, the second ring had not appeared on Ayling's finger, and thus Bolt's team would concentrate on capital cities to find the jeweller who had used wrong solder. It certainly seemed now that the jeweller would be found—if alive after all these years—in a near-by town like Geelong or Colac, even in Lorne.

Despite the storm, Bony slept soundly and late, waking to see the sun trying to stand still upon the racing clouds and the trees about the hotel attempting to fly. At breakfast Mrs. Washfold told him that the roads to Anglesea and Lorne were blocked by landslides and that it was expected traffic would be halted for two days. After breakfast he decided on a tramp to the sea, and, of course, Stug accompanied him.

He made another decision shortly after leaving the hotel. To look down upon a stormy sea from a height is to miss much of its majesty and everything of its power, and he chose, therefore, to visit the beach.

The road was clean, and the gutters still ran water following a rainfall of over four inches. The wind slid across the headland, slid over and about Bony like a pervious glacier and almost as cold. The colour of the lighthouse was off-white, and the coast towards invisible Lorne was stained dirty yellow by the spume.

Something tremendous had happened to the inlet. The winding creek was five times as broad, and when he reached it at the Picnic Ground there were more water birds than he had ever seen there. The creek was flowing inward, and much of the sand bar had been eaten away by the pounding surf. Each charging wave broke far out, rushed to charge the sand bar and empty most of its content over it into the creek.

The temper of the sea was vile. The wind raised a sandblast to sting Bony's face and slam pain against the dog's nose, and when they reached the beach and Bony paused to watch the cataracts of water emptying into the inlet, Stug promptly sat with his back to the sea and shut fast his eyes.

The mark left by high tide was plain, as the tide was ebbing, and but here and there did it lie at the feet of the cliffs. At the main point the black rocks boiled in the cauldron off the little beach where the dead penguin had come ashore, and Bony walked with effort along the sand to reach it.

He came again to the funnel in the cliff face where, as previously, the debris was in the power of perpetual motion. The stinging spray forced him to turn up his coat collar and Stug to proceed at an absurd angle. Strongly elemental, Bony feared the elements, and, fearing, was fascinated. Here the sea's fury was awe-inspiring.

Hate controlled the sea, and hate burnished the dull-gold faces of the cliffs. Other than the man and dog, nothing lived along this battleground where motion contended with frozen implacability. When the lighthouse came into view it held no association with the scene, reminding Bony of a picture of a patrician lady gazing above the heads of the screaming rabble.

Coming to the beach where he had buried the penguin, his mind was wholly enthralled by the pitiless striving of giants, and there, as once before he had stood with his back to the sea, he gazed upward at the point where Mary Wessex had appeared.

Clearly he remembered the configuration of the cliff edge against the sky, and he saw now proof that the place where Mary Wessex struggled with Dick Lake was within a yard of the upper end of the ledge down which he had sidled to reach the cave. He could even see the ledge—knowing now it was there to be seen—and could visually follow it to the overhang. There was no possible doubt that had he succumbed to the blow he had received on that ledge, he would not have survived the fall. He would have dropped like a stone down the yellow face to the rubble at its chin. To lie there . . . there . . .

An object dark and foreign lay just where he would have lain, and with the dog at heel, he strode up the shelving sand to investigate.

It was a young man dressed in working clothes. On his feet were rubber-soled shoes. He lay broken and still, and his face was toward Bony. The face was unmarked, the grey eyes wide.

Bony gazed upon Dick Lake, his throat constricted, all experience failing to control the rising horror, for he had grown to like this once casual and happy man.

TRAGEDY AT SPLIT POINT

The dog crept forward and sniffed at the body. It then slunk away, sat and howled. A cloud passed from the sun, and the light, pouring through the spume, laid gold to the rocks and gilded the dead face.

Automatically, Bony noted the time. Training beat upon and submerged natural reactions.

Lake had worn no overcoat when he fell, and he had turned up the collar of his working coat and fastened it with a safety pin. The clothes were as wet as though immersed in the sea. There was no watch to give the time of the fall, and nothing whatever in the pockets save a quantity of strong, light rope.

Bony sat on a rock and gazed at Stug, and Stug lifted his head and wept at the passing of one of his many friends. During the dark night, or at early break of day, Dick Lake had ventured down the ledge to reach the pirate's cave to find if Mr. Rawlings had removed the clothes and shoes and suitcase, and, if not, to dispose of them at some other place.

Either he had slipped or the rain-sodden ledge had given way. Proof of his intention to visit the cave rested with rope in a pocket and rubber-soled canvas shoes on the feet.

For no other reason than the marked difference between finding the body of a person unknown to you and that of a man with whom you have laughed, Bony removed his overcoat and placed it over the body of Dick Lake, weighting the corners with stones. Feeling the lack of the coat, he walked as smartly as the beach sand would permit to the inlet, and finally up to the lighthouse and to the cliff. Flat on his chest, he peered over the edge, observing that the ledge now ended several feet short of the overhang and that the rain had removed all traces of the breakaway.

Walking up the highway to the hotel, he went over the events culminating in this tragedy, and he pondered on the probable motive prompting Lake to retrieve the murdered man's effects despite the hazards. Again he saw Lake with Fred Ayling walking from the latter's camp to the first of the wood stacks, and the following conversation most likely took place:

"When I was leaving the Wessex homestead last afternoon," Ayling said, "Mary came after me, telling me that the feller at the pub, Rawlings, had found our old cave."

"Crikey!" exploded Lake. "What happened?"

"She told me she'd been watching him. Couldn't tell me why. Said he went down the ledge, and that she lay down on the cliff and waited for him to come up. He was down there a long time. When he came up, she bashed him with a rock—when his head was about level with the cliff edge. Seems that she ran away, believing that she'd knocked Rawlings off the ledge."

"And she didn't . . . knock him off . . . couldn't have."

"That's about it, Dick. He must have hung on in spite of the blow. Reckon Mary's clear on that point."

"He musta found them clothes and suitcase," said the now alarmed Lake. "Was he bringing anything up with him, did Mary say?"

"She said she didn't think he was. I kept asking her about that."

"Sounds crook, don't it?" was Lake's opinion, and Ayling said:

"Rawlings isn't what he's making out to be. More'n likely he's a detective."

"Yair. What beats me is how he came to find out about the cave. Did Mary say?"

"No, she didn't. But he had Bert Washfold's dog with him. She saw Stug with Rawlings when he went down, and he was coming up the ledge after him. The dog could have put him wise to the cave."

"Yes, crook all right, Fred. What do we do now, d'you reckon?"

"You go down for those clothes and things as soon as you can. If they're all there as you left 'em, there's not much harm done. If any of them, or all of them, are gone, then Rawlings must have taken them."

"All right, I'll shift 'em tonight. Hell! What rotten luck. And our old cave the best possible place, too. Did Mary tell you when she conked Rawlings with the rock?"

"No. Couldn't get that from her. What worries me, and makes

me think he's a d., is that he never said anything about being hit."

"Never showed no mark on his conk that I noticed," vowed Lake. "Mary musta been mistaken. Anyhow, I'll fix it about them clothes."

That appeared to be the basis of Dick Lake's foolhardy attempt to negotiate the rain-sodden ledge in the middle of the stormy night, for he had gone down the ledge before six that mornnig, when the rain had stopped.

In the hotel Bony found Moss Way with the licensee.

"Happened to have seen Dick?" Moss asked.

"Why?" evaded Bony.

"Wasn't in camp when I woke up," replied Way, obviously perturbed. "That was early, too."

"Ever walk in his sleep, d'you know?"

"Him! Sleeps like a dog without fleas. Like me. Why?"

"He must have sleepwalked last night. He fell over the cliff opposite the lighthouse. I went along the beach to the Point and found him under the cliff. Been dead for hours, I think."

"You sure it's Dick?" demanded Way, and Bony nodded and sipped whisky and soda.

"Why I asked if he ever walked in his sleep was because he was wearing no overcoat over his working clothes and was wearing canvas tennis shoes. Another drink, please."

"Well, that beats hell!" exclaimed Washfold. "You look cold, Mr. Rawlings. Didn't you take an overcoat this morning?"

"Yes. I placed it over the body. I think you had better ring through to the police."

"Yes, I suppose so."

The licensee rolled away to the telephone, and Way said:

"Decent . . . to leave your coat over him." He eyed Bony steadily, and with difficulty controlled his voice. "Me and Dick's been cobbers ever since he came back from the war. Good bloke, all right. Never groused, never argued, never shirked his share of work. I can't believe what you're telling us."

"Did you know him before the war?"

"No. I come from Port Campbell. His old woman will be upset, and his pa. Good sorts, the Lakes. I'm havin' another drink. What about you?"

Way lifted the counter flap and poured the drinks, leaving a florin on the counter. Bony was feeling warmer when Washfold returned to say that Staley would try to get through as soon as possible, in view of the landslides, and would have to use a bicycle.

"Said as to leave the body where it is until he gets here," supplemented Washfold.

Bony looked doubtful, for it was necessary to keep Moss Way from his camp until Staley did arrive.

"Tide was high last night," he said. "Up to within a dozen feet of the body. Could come higher still this afternoon."

"It will that," agreed Washfold, and Way said:

"Blast the police. We'll go for Dick now. Only right and proper. Who'll tell his ma and pa? Not on the telephone, are they?"

"No," replied Washfold. "But the Wessexes are. Alfie could ride over with the news from there. Creeks can't be that bad."

"Alfie would swim a horse acrost the creeks, Bert. You phone Mrs. Wessex now. Then we'll take your truck down as far as the Picnic Ground. Have to make a sort of stretcher, too."

It was one o'clock before the body was brought to the old schoolhouse, and four o'clock when Staley arrived with Dr. Close. The policeman grumbled at the disobedience to his orders, examined the body, received the doctor's report, and sought Mr. Rawlings for a statement.

"Funny business, sir, isn't it?"

"Yes, strange," agreed Bony. "As I have no explanation to offer at this stage, we could say that the dead man possibly met his death whilst walking in his sleep."

"Long way to walk. And such a night," objected Staley stiffly.

"I won't argue, Senior," Bony said gently. "He had light rope with him. I took that when I found him. I know where he was going when he fell. We will stick to somnambulism. I'd like you to go at once to Lake's camp and impound his effects, among which may be the answer. You could stay the night here, and so put the things in your room, and we could go through them later. Take the Super's car."

"Very well, sir."

For the rest of the day Bony kept from public gaze, and during dinner that night, taken with Staley, he learned that the Lakes had arrived and that Mrs. Penwarden had insisted on putting them up.

"In view of the doctor's opinion," Staley said, "I let them have the body. Tom Owen brought a coffin from Penwarden's workshop. The old man came with it. Mrs. Wessex helped him with the body. The old identities around here weren't slow in claiming one of their own. What did you think of young Lake?"

"Good type, Staley. The smile hid much, you know. You impounded his possessions?"

"In my room. The key's in my pocket."

Mrs. Washfold came in with pork cutlets on a tray and tears on her unadorned cheeks. She said nothing, and they gave her no opportunity for emotional relief. She and her husband were abed when Bony entered Staley's room.

"Well, what have we?"

"A tin trunk, a suitcase, and a kit bag, sir."

"Good! We'll begin with the kit bag."

The bag contained nothing but working clothes and a pair of old shoes. As Staley replaced these things, Bony offered no comment. The suitcase was small, and its contents were next lifted and placed on the bed.

It contained two new shirts, several pairs of unworn socks, three soiled linen collars, a writing pad and a fountain pen, and a bankbook. The bankbook showed a credit of five hundred and forty-seven pounds. Under the cover of the writing pad were two letters addressed to the dead man by a woman in Geelong. They were innocuous. Engraved on the gold band about the pen was the data: "To D.L. from S.P.P.S., 1939."

"Nothing so far," commented Bony.

"Expect much, sir?"

"A gold signet ring engraved with the letters B.B."

The suitcase joined the kit bag in a corner of the room, and Staley opened the lid of the tin trunk, an old-fashioned, well-made receptacle. The first article lifted to the bed was the heavy blue overcoat Lake had worn for the trip to Geelong with Ayling and "the mob." Then followed the suit and the shoes he had worn that evening. More shirts, both used and new, came to light, and a pair of expensive gloves never worn and still within the gift box in which they had been bought.

"This might be interesting," Staley said, setting on the bed an object wrapped in tissue paper.

Bony removed the paper, and the light was reflected by the honey-coloured, brilliantly polished surface of a flattish square box. Lifting it, Bony murmured:

"No visible joins. Penwarden's work for sure."

He raised the lid and found that the contents were wrapped in tissue paper. There was a wristlet watch of good quality, a New Testament on the flyleaf of which was inscribed: "For Dick from Mum and Pop Wessex. To keep always in his tunic pocket that he will be armoured against all enemies and often reminded of those who pray for him."

"Fine woman," said Staley.

"Agreed. Young Lake certainly valued highly gifts he received. This lighter . . . never been used. Ah! Might be photographs."

The paper was removed to reveal photographs pasted to cheap mounts. All were of soldiers, save one in which a sailor appeared. Lake was included in every group, Ayling in one, and Eldred Wessex in two. These pictures Bony put aside.

"Casual about renewing his driver's licence, and particular with gifts from friends," Staley eventually agreed with Bony. "The type never varies."

He brought up another suit, a sports coat and grey flannel trousers, a pair of new shoes, a tennis racket having a broken string, and a red-and-white football guernsey with the figure 5 emblazoned on the back.

"Played for Geelong?" questioned Bony.

"Not Geelong's colours. Local team."

"This local team—go far to play matches?"

"Oh yes. Warrnambool, Colac, Point Lonsdale."

Staley brought up a worn copy of the *Union Jack Magazine,* featuring Sexton Blake and his boy assistant, Tinker; a copy of the *Argus,* on the front page of which was a picture of marching troops and, written in ink, "Good old 7th Divi"; a Japanese soldier's tunic;

a Malay kris, and, accompanied by an expletive from Staley, a revolver.

"A thirty-two," Staley said, glancing down the barrel. He broke it open and looked through the barrel pointed at the light. "Been fired since it was last cleaned. Man in lighthouse killed with a thirty-two."

"Put it aside," ordered Bony, pleased that Staley proved to be no novice when handling the weapon to preserve possible prints. "What next?"

"'Looks like a lot of old letters."

There could be thirty letters, all addressed to Lake, care the Post Office, Split Point, and Bony sorted them in accordance with the calligraphy of the writers whilst noting the postal-date stamp. This done, he said:

"Have a smoke, Senior, while I go through these." A half hour passed, when he said: "None posted prior to the end of the war, and the majority of no use to us. But, Staley, there are letters from Eldred Wessex and letters from a girl signing herself Jean Stebbings, and these are certainly of interest. First the letters written by Eldred Wessex.

"The story of Eldred Wessex reads like this. In June 1946, Eldred wrote from Sydney saying he had informed his parents of his intention to go to America to make a wad of dough—to use his own phrase. It's evident that Lake wrote urging him to return home before going. In December of the same year Eldred wrote saying he was back again in Sydney, that the trip to America was a failure, and that he was doing fairly well with a valuable agency which demanded his close attention.

"From his letters it's obvious that Lake repeatedly urged him to come home, but Wessex presents one excuse after another. Nothing in his letter reveals the nature of his business activities in Sydney.

"There are four letters addressed to Lake by a girl in Sydney who signs her name as Jean Stebbings. The dates of these letters all follow the discovery of our lighthouse murder. Jean Stebbings is concerned about the whereabouts of Eldred Wessex, who left her on the morning of February twenty-sixth. Her next letter indicates that Lake had not seen or heard from Eldred Wessex. Her last letter was posted on March twenty-sixth, and again the writer infers she had heard from Lake that Eldred Wessex had not turned up at Split Point."

"Eldred Wessex is important, sir?" asked the baffled Staley.

"It would seem so, Senior. Put all those things back in the trunk and we'll go to bed. I'll keep the letters, the photographs, and the gun. When is the funeral?"

"Tomorrow. You want the inquest delayed a bit?"

"Yes. You can release Lake's possessions to his parents." Bony lit a cigarette and pensively watched Staley. "I'm not liking this. A detective should earn his clues by exercising his brain."

"Meaning, sir?"

"I don't like clues to come to me through the death of a man who might have risked his life to save a pal."

TWO WOMEN

Bony flew to Sydney, where he paid his respects to the Chief of the New South Wales C.I.B. and gained willing co-operation.

A police car took him out to Ashfield at ten in the morning, an unfortunate hour for a lady whose habits are irregular. The house at which the car stopped was charming, the front door being protected by a finely wrought iron grille with the bell centred unobtrusively amid the petals of an ornamental flower.

An elderly woman answered the summons and, on sighting the d.s., instantly betrayed irritation. Upon being requested to inform her mistress they wished to interview her, she conducted them to a restfully furnished lounge. There they sat for twenty-five minutes before Opal Jane appeared.

If Opal Jane was displeased, she didn't show it. She was dainty, vivacious, dark, and distinctly beautiful, and dressed with that sort of simplicity which means dollars in any man's language. She smiled coolly at the detective sergeant and, with interest not wholly feigned, regarded the man who looked like a rajah in civvies.

The detective sergeant presented Bony quite creditably. Opal Jane's demeanour was unchanged.

"I never rise before eleven, Inspector Bonaparte. I suppose you've come to ask more and more questions. I'm beginning to wish I'd never met that wretched man."

"Our friends are sometimes most embarrassing," Bony murmured, holding a match to her cigarette. "I hate having to talk shop with you, and would prefer to discuss books and flowers. You knew the late Thomas Baker for how long?"

The violet eyes hardened.

"Surely you are not going to ask the same questions, Inspector Bonaparte," she said. "I knew Baker for about five years. In that time he's called on me about seven or eight times. As I've told the sergeant, Baker was a second steward on a liner."

"You were really unaware that he traded in imitation pearls and other things?"

"I certainly was. I don't associate with crooks."

Bony nodded as though pleased that so unpleasant a subject was finished.

"Tell me, what kind of a man was Baker . . . personality?"

"Oh! A good sort, Inspector. He could play around. Free with his money, and not one to be upset over trifles."

"Expensive tastes?"

"Yes, he liked the best of everything."

"Did it never occur to you that his salary as second steward, even on a first-class liner, would barely meet his expenditures?"

"No . . . o."

"I understand that he presented you with several most expensive opals, that he took you often to exclusive night clubs."

Opal June smiled.

"You're not deliberately being naïve, Inspector?"

"Perhaps I am being natural. Thomas Baker could have been in receipt of a private income. Your friendship with him was . . . platonic?"

"He wanted to marry me. They all do. As to the source of his income, I never concern myself about the financial affairs of my friends . . . excepting their ability with a chequebook."

"Is one of your friends named Eldred Wessex?"

Opal Jane shook her head, and Bony was satisfied that Eldred Wessex was not one of her clientele. Still, a name often conveys nothing. From his wallet he took the picture of Eldred Wessex, hatless and standing with five other soldiers. Everything bar the head of Wessex he had obliterated with India ink.

"Have you ever seen that man?" he asked, proffering the picture.

Violet eyes clashed with blue eyes, and the woman realised that in this dark man all her feminine artifice would profit her nothing.

Opal Jane carried the picture to the window. The detective sergeant looked bored. Bonaparte admired a painting of a ship under full sail. The woman returned to her chair before speaking.

"I don't know why I should answer your last question," she said. "I had nothing to do with Baker's murder, and I don't want to be mixed up with it."

"Surely I may assume that, having been friendly with Baker, you do not wish his murderer to escape the legal penalty? Or have you something still hidden from us? Forgive the implication, but I cannot evade it."

"I've nothing to hide. I want to be left in peace. Yes, I've seen this man. Once when I was dining with Tom Baker at the Blue Mist. He came to our table and spoke to Tom. Another time Tom and I were going out to Randwick and he stopped for a moment to speak as we were about to get into a taxi. I don't know his name. And Tom Baker never referred to him."

"When was it you last saw him?"

"Before Christmas . . . in November, I think it was."

"At the two meetings of those men, did they appear friendly?"

"Yes, in an offhand way. I'd say they were acquaintances rather than friends. They were quite pleasant to each other."

Bony rose, and Opal Jane smilingly rose with him.

"Have you done with me, Inspector? So soon?"

"Unfortunately, yes," Bony blandly told her. "It was good of you to receive us so early. I've been surreptitiously admiring that painting, and the bookcase which is quite a treasure."

"I'm glad you like my bits, Inspector. My father was an alcoholic and my mother died from cocaine. The home . . . you can imagine.

What life withheld from the child the woman has squeezed from it."

In the hall Bony remarked:

"Your passion for opals is something I can understand. Pearls! Do you like pearls?"

Opal Jane smiled most sweetly.

"I never refuse pearls, Inspector. Sawyer and White have a lovely string at five hundred guineas—if you happen to be interested. And I'll promise to keep them for a little while. You see, I prefer opals, knowing something about them. Pearls I always sell for cash."

The sergeant opened the front door, and still Bony lingered.

"D'you know if Thomas Baker had a second Christian name?"

"I never heard of it."

"Or a pet name—a nickname?"

"No. He was always Tom to me."

"Thank you." Bony smiled and reached the doorstep. "Favour me by pronouncing the letter T, will you?"

Opal Jane obliged.

"Now the letter B."

Again the woman complied, and again Bony blandly smiled and wished her good-bye.

In the police car which was taking them to Coogee, he asked:

"Did you note any similarity in the pronunciation of the letters T and B?"

"Yes, faintly, I think," replied the sergeant.

They left the car at a huge block of flats, and the sergeant rang the bell of Number 47. A young woman appeared in dishabille and escorted by the aroma of frying sausages. Her brown eyes lit with interest in Bony, and hardened at the sight of the sergeant, whose civilian clothes were no disguise.

"What is it?" she demanded briskly.

"Are you Jean Stebbings?" asked Bony.

"I am. What d'you want?"

"We are police officers, Miss Stebbings. Will you invite us inside? I want to ask a few questions."

"All right! Come in. In there, please. I'll turn off the gas."

They found themselves in a tiny sitting room, and when the girl entered she had attended to her hair and face. The shrewd sergeant assessed her correctly. Bony persuaded her to be seated, saying:

"You know a man named Eldred Wessex, do you not?"

"Yes," she replied, barely above a whisper, to add fiercely: "Go on. Tell me. I like it quick."

"When did you last see him?"

"See him! Why, weeks ago. What's happened to him?"

"Nothing that I'm aware of. What is he to you?"

The girl fought and temporarily conquered her anxiety, Bony patiently waiting. Her clasped hands stilled their agitation, and he noted the wedding ring. She lifted her head, as though with pride, and a blush stirred under her skin.

"Eldred is—was—my man. We're going to be married someday." The fears returned. "Where is he? Why don't you tell me where he is?"

"Don't you know?"

"Would I be asking you?"

"Dick Lake doesn't know, either."

"So he told me. Before he walked off a cliff. I seen that in the papers."

"What made you write to Dick about Eldred?" pressed Bony.

"Dick was his friend. Eldred came from Split Point. They were in the war together. But you know all that. You know more, too. What's happened to Eldred? Go on, tell me."

"I know neither where he is nor what's happened to him, if anything," Bony said quietly. "I am seeking your aid to locate him."

"All right! Then what's he done?"

"Other people as well as you are anxious to know where Eldred Wessex is," Bony continued quietly. "It's my job to trace missing persons. Dozens of people are reported missing every year. Many fade away purposely. What work did Wessex do here in Sydney?"

"Something to do with Security Service, so he told me. Said it suited him because he felt so restless after the army life. But—I wrote to Security Service, and they sent a man here to tell me they didn't know anything about him."

"How long have you known him?"

"Just a year."

"Did he have any friends in Sydney?"

"Not that I know of."

"Acquaintances, then?"

"A few, yes."

"Was this man one of them?" Bony softly asked.

The girl accepted the picture, glanced at it, dropped it to the floor. She startled even the stolid sergeant.

"He didn't! He didn't! He didn't do it!" she cried shrilly.

"What on earth are you talking about, Miss Stebbings?" asked Bony, and she answered accusingly:

"That's the man in the bath. That's the man they found murdered in the lighthouse. Eldred never did that, I tell you. He never went back to Split Point. Dick Lake told me. Kept on telling me Eldred never went home."

"You recognise this man, though, the man found in the lighthouse?"

"Yes. No, I don't. I've never seen him."

The tortured face was defiant, and Bony guessed at the battle being fought by this woman to remove the load of suspicion from her mind, a battle which had been proceeding since Eldred Wessex left her. Gently he said:

"Wouldn't it be better for you to know the truth about Eldred? To know why he went away, why he hasn't written, instead of going on from day to day worrying yourself sick about him?"

The woman's face was like a vase suddenly overtaken by centuries of time. She broke into a storm of weeping, burying her face in a handkerchief, both hands to the handkerchief. The wedding ring was too large. It swivelled round her finger. It wasn't a wedding ring.

"Let us try to unearth the truth, Miss Stebbings," Bony urged. "Not to know will always be worse than knowing. Who was the man murdered in the lighthouse?"

"Eldred called him Tommy," moaned the girl. "He came here once with Eldred. Eldred said he was in Security Service too. Then he called in the afternoon of the day Eldred went away. He came asking for Eldred, and I said he was out. He didn't come again after that."

"What was the date?"

The watchful detective sergeant noticed the iron in Bony's voice, and wondered at the placidity of expression as they waited through another outburst of grief. Bony produced a second picture.

"Is this your Eldred?"

She dabbed at her eyes. Bony looked at the ring. She gazed at the picture of Wessex shown to Opal Jane and slowly nodded. Bony passed the picture to the detective sergeant and waited for the girl to regain something of composure. It was the sergeant who asked the next question:

"D'you know a man called Waghorn?"

"No. Only heard about him. Never seen him. Never want to."

"Wessex say anything about Waghorn?"

"Never."

"When did Eldred leave you—the date—Miss Stebbings?" proceeded Bony.

"On my birthday. It was my birthday. Eldred left home after breakfast, saying he would be bringing me a string of pearls. He never did. He never came back."

"What is your birth date?"

"February twenty-sixth."

Bony stood up to leave. Bending over the girl, he patted her shoulder.

"We'll find your man, Miss Stebbings. Did he give you that ring?"

"No. He let me wear it until he could give me a wedding ring."

SWAPPING CLUES

At five minutes after four o'clock Bony arrived at the Melbourne airport; at five minutes to five he was seated opposite the officer in charge of Military Records. On the desk was an opened file.

"Wessex, Eldred," murmured the officer, and detailed the unit, rank, number, dates of enlistment and discharge. "Seems to have been troublesome, Inspector."

"I thought it probable. Serious trouble?" prompted Bony.

"Disorderly conduct. Ah, striking a superior officer. A charge of theft from a forward canteen. Found not guilty by court-martial. Received a hundred days for grievously injuring a comrade in a mix-up at Port Moresby. Was recommended for the Military Medal at that time, and the recommendation withdrawn. Was returned to Australia to serve that sentence. Seems to have been no damn good."

"But was recommended for the M.M."

"Sometimes goes that way, Inspector. Some men never make soldiers but are excellent fighters."

"H'm! Revealing. This man Wessex served with a friend of his named Dick Lake. Could I ask you for Lake's record?"

"Certainly. I'll send for it." A bell button was pressed, and the order given to a clerk. "Lake! Haven't I read his name in the paper recently? Ah, yes. I recall it. Down at Split Point, wasn't it? Lovely place. Spent a holiday there a year or two ago. Thanks, Simms."

The clerk again withdrew, and the officer opened the file on Dick Lake.

"Lake, Richard. Fairly clean record. A number of small offences, such as being A.W.O.L., slovenly on parade, disobeying an order. All offences committed in the training camp. Ah . . . thought to be associated with Eldred Wessex on the canteen charge. Didn't stop him from gaining a decoration, though. D.C.M."

"Distinguished Conduct Medal!"

"An award well worth having." The officer chuckled. "Court-martialled for refusing to accept promotion. I know the type. If I had a division of men like that, there's no war I wouldn't win."

On leaving Military Records, Bony hailed a taxi, and at the third hotel at which he called he obtained a room. The price rocked him, but then Bolt would have to pass payment. He descended to the dining room wearing his best suit, was welcomed by the head-waiter with unusual effusiveness and conducted to a table for two as far as possible from the band. He was studying the menu when Superintendent Bolt dropped like a stone from the ceiling into the opposite chair.

"Been getting around, eh?" Bolt said, small brown eyes boring like gimlets. "Clear soup for me, and sole Marnier followed by wine trifle and black coffee with a brandy."

"Off the diet?" calmly inquired Bony.

"Don't believe in starving the old body. Get much from Sydney?"

Bony sighed.

"And they promised not to press-agent me," he complained.

"They didn't. You were picked up coming off the plane, tracked to Military Records, then via the Australia, Menzies, and so to this pub. I then contacted the manager, who's a pal of mine. Elementary, Bony my boy, elementary. I'll be waiting for you to give when the coffee and brandy arrive."

"A spot of trading, Super? The brandy might give us the confidence to swap clues. As you will be paying for the brandy, see to it that it's the best."

"And me saving up for a new car. What a hope! Call on Opal Jane?"

"I thought we were to wait for the coffee. Yes, I did."

"Opinion?"

"A lovely lady," replied Bony, and Bolt searched and found no subtlety.

"Wish I had her dough," he said. "Wish I wasn't so ruddy fat."

"Sydney has her well taped," Bony said. "The list of her gentlemen friends would astonish you. Know a man named Waghorn?"

The small brown eyes appeared to pivot round to search the card index in the domed head.

"No, can't say that I do. Where does he fit in?"

"Waghorn is a small-time crook operating in Sydney. Suspected of being mixed up with smuggling. I'd rather like to talk to him about the weather."

"Yeah, stormy weather," Bolt said, and chuckled. "This Waghorn character do the lighthouse killing?"

"He may be able to tell us something about it, Super. Perhaps you would assist me by having him brought in."

"Anything you want, Bony, anything. My Commish is becoming annoyed at our failure to come up with results. You ask Sydney to pick him up?"

"No. I left that to you. Detective Sergeant Eulo knows the man well. Your opposite number in Sydney agreed not to divulge my operations in Sydney, but I told him you would become interested in Waghorn."

Superintendent Bolt patted the marble dome rising from the fringe of grey hair about his ears. It could have been done to shoo a fly, but there were no flies.

"Want this Waghorn brought to Melbourne?" he asked.

"Yes. If he is still in New South Wales. I think it likely, however, that he's in Victoria. Of course, he may be in South Australia, or down at the South Pole. I want him."

"You'll have him, boots and all. Still interested in that signet ring?"

Without the slightest pause, Bony replied casually:

"Yes. It might give something fresh about Thomas Baker. Did you find the jeweller?"

"Lives down at Point Lonsdale. Retired in '42 from the business he had at Colac. His assistant bought the business. Says he remembers making the mistake about the solder but can't say who bought the ring. Said his late boss might have some record of it, and gave us his address. Info only came in a minute before I left the office this evening."

"Have you done anything further about it?"

"No. Thought you might want to interview that jeweller."

"I do." Bony smiled his thanks. "There are three rings exactly alike. The one found in the murdered man's overcoat. Another on the finger of a champion axeman. The third on the finger of a woman in Sydney. There is a fourth ring, I think, although I haven't yet come across it."

Bolt was generous enough to smile his thanks. He chanced a question:

"Found out what the letters B.B. mean?"

"Oh yes. Some time ago. Bully Buccaneers."

"Enlightening."

"Ship Steward Thomas Baker ordered his suit with the Adelaide tailor, and paid cash there and then. The tailor thought he said B. Baker when recording his name. Actually he must have said T. Baker."

"Nice point."

"Had the transaction been such that the suit was to be paid for on delivery, the tailor would have been more alert. The Bully Buccaneers were a crew of pirates who sailed the Caribbean and captured treasure ships, conveying as passengers ladies old and bent who possessed much gold and many fine jewels. As I mentioned, I have located three of these Bully Buccaneers."

The Chief of the Victoria C.I.B. grinned, for his eyes threatened to shrivel the soul of Napoleon Bonaparte.

"Your lucidity continues to claim my admiration. Our friend in the preserving tank—he's being decently buried tomorrow—was a reincarnation of Captain Morgan. So what?"

"He wasn't a member of the pirate crew. What happened was that a member of the pirate crew removed the watch from the dead man's wrist and put it in a pocket of the raincoat. The ring on his own finger was broken and slipped off. One can imagine the haste in which the body was stripped."

"Another nice point, Bony. I suppose you wouldn't care to add a few supplementary remarks?"

"I fear I am not yet in that happy position," Bony said blandly. "Should the jeweller I interview tomorrow be able to remember to whom he sold those signet rings engraved with the letters B.B., I will have advanced another step. When you pick up Waghorn, I may advance a further step."

Bolt frowned, heaved a silent sigh.

"As muddy as all that, eh? That feller Lake, who fell over the cliff. Have anything to do with the murder, or was he bumped off?"

"Lake could have been walking in his sleep," Bony said without smiling.

"Bad habit. Lots of murders committed by fellers walking in their sleep."

Bolt betrayed impatience only in the manner in which he struck a match to his cigar. It says much for Bony that the vast man's confidence grew rather than diminished, and much for Bolt that Bony implicitly trusted him not to make moves beyond those agreed to.

"That gun Staley sent us certainly fired the fatal bullet," Bolt contributed. "Has Lake's fingerprints on it. I didn't have Staley tell us where you found that weapon."

"Among Lake's effects. Any other prints beside his?"

Bolt stared. He pursed his lips and emitted a thin stream of smoke.

"No. Did you expect others?"

"Yes and no. Had there been prints additional to those of Lake, my reasoning would have been faulty."

"Lake, then, was the murderer?"

"I don't know—yet. Greed and loyalty, bitterness and love, viciousness and altruism are some of the ingredients of this mystery.

"High up in the face of the cliff at Split Point is a cave, discovered years ago by small boys. It is so difficult to approach that none but those boys ever knew of it until I found it. It was in the cave that I discovered the murdered man's clothes and suitcase. It was whilst coming up from it to the cliff top that I was hit with a stone. When he fell, Lake was going down the face of the cliff to find out if I had removed the clothes and, if not, to transfer them elsewhere. He made the attempt in the middle of the night, when it was raining torrents, when the wind blew a gale.

"I like to think, Super, that Dick Lake died in the attempt to remove evidence which would condemn a pal, not himself. He was one of those three boys I mentioned. The others were in it too: a Fred Ayling and an Eldred Wessex. Eldred Wessex is known in Sydney as Waghorn. We want him to give an account of his movements on and about the date of the lighthouse killing. He went out of circulation two days before Baker was shot. He and Baker were acquaintances at least."

"Do we grill this Waghorn when we net him?" asked Bolt.

"I would prefer to do that, as I hold several threads."

"This other bloke, Ayling?"

"The Captain of the Bully Buccaneers! Leave him to me, Super."

On passing through Geelong, Bony deviated to Point Lonsdale, where he called on Mr. Letchfield, who, in 1942, had decided to spend the rest of his life watching the ships passing through Port Phillip Heads.

"I am informed that Mr. Cummins bought your business in Colac, and it was he who suggested you may be able to assist me with a line of inquiry I am conducting," Bony said, having announced his name and position.

"Certainly, Inspector," agreed the rotund jeweller. "I am all attention."

"It appears that when Mr. Cummins was your assistant he made a mistake due to inexperience as a goldsmith. When altering an eighteen-carat gold ring for a customer, he used nine-carat solder. Can you recall that incident?"

"Quite well. I remember it clearly, Inspector. Poor Cummins was most remorseful. As you said, he was then an indifferent goldsmith, although, mind you, he was an artist with watches and settings."

"It is not, then, a common mistake?"

"Only a very young apprentice would make such an error. My word, it all comes back to me. I was very busy, and having removed the necessary segment, I asked Cummins to solder it. I should have pointed out that the solder must be, like the ring, eighteen-carat."

"Can you recall the date, approximately?" pressed Bony. "Mr. Cummins is unable to unearth the record of the transaction."

The jeweller pondered so long that Bony was anticipating disappointment.

"Y . . . es, Inspector. It was in August or early September '38. There was a festival or something at the time, which was why I was busy."

"Not a football match?"

"Ah, yes, that was it. It was the final of the Western District Football League. Colac played Split Point, and won. Of course, that was it. The customer . . . Actually there were three of them, three young men from the Split Point team. They wanted to look at signet rings, and insisted that the rings must be all alike. I was able to show them rings of a standard make and design which they finally chose. And then what d'you think they wanted?"

"To have them engraved alike?"

Mr. Letchfield's bushy eyebrows shot upward.

"Remarkable, Inspector. Yes, they wanted each ring to be engraved with the letters B.B. I remember asking them what the letters stood for, as they had no relationship with the team to which the young men belonged. They wouldn't tell me. Fidgeted, looked sheepish, as young men sometimes will. Then came the difficulty. I was able to suit two of the customers but did not have a ring to fit the finger of the third young man. And so, as they were remaining in Colac overnight, I told them I would have the third ring ready by the next morning.

"I cut out the segment and gave it over to Cummins, and he completed the work before we shut the shop. The next morning, when the three young men came, I took the ring from my drawer, gave it a final polish before presenting it to the customer . . . and saw Cummins' mistake.

"I confess, Inspector, that I was horrified not so much by the mistake itself but at the discovery being made so late. I pointed out the mistake to the customer and said I would have another ring ready for him by twelve. To that, he said they were leaving Colac under the hour, and he insisted that the slight and narrow variation of colour didn't matter. So I allowed him to take it."

"Do you remember their names, Mr. Letchfield?" Bony asked.

"No. No, I can't remember their names, that is to say, the name of each individual. But I do remember that, a week or so later, I received an order from Split Point for another ring of the same design to be engraved with the same letters. On a piece of paper accompanying the order was drawn in pencil the size of the required ring, evidently done by running a pencil point round a ring pressed to the paper.

"There was an oddity about that order which fixed it in my memory. The customer signed himself Eldred Wessex, and wrote from Split Point. The ring he required was far too small for the finger of a man, so this one was evidently meant for a lady's hand. I fulfilled the order."

"You did not receive any subsequent orders?"

"No."

"Or engrave the letters B.B. on any piece of jewellery for a customer?"

Bony was pleased that Letchfield hesitated to answer before being sure. He stated that never, subsequently, had he engraved those letters on any article of jewellery, and having warmly thanked him, Bony left.

He lunched at the hotel at the pretty little hamlet of Barwon Heads, and it was after four when the old single-seater chugged up the rise to the Post-Office-Store at Split Point. The now familiar scene was dulled by rain, and beyond the great inlet the coast headlands were but a degree darker than the slate-grey sea.

For a second or two he felt like the prodigal returning home, and then he became a stoat confronted by a rabbit burrow, a fastidious stoat having a predilection for a black rabbit. This stoat knew every passage, every circus, every cul-de-sac of this warren. He knew every brown rabbit inhabiting this warren . . . but the black one he had never seen.

When Bony left Melbourne that morning, the police in every capital city had been requested to bring in a man known as Waghorn, and recognised by Detective Sergeant Eulo when presented with the picture of Eldred Wessex. Waghorn was known to the Sydney C.I.B. Consorting Squad as a man moving on the edge of gangland, a man long suspected of unlawful practices but not to date enmeshed in the law's net.

Nothing was known against the woman who hoped to marry him, and inquiries conducted after Bony had questioned her produced the telegraphed report that Jean Stebbings was of good repute to several responsible people who had known her for years. The report confirmed Bony's opinion that Wessex had withheld from her his activities as Waghorn and confided his background as Eldred Wessex.

Why had this man not returned home after war service? Had he been forbidden to return by a father who had learned of the gaol sentence he had served as a soldier? Was the story of his going to America a fabrication issued by his parents to account for the son's absence?

On February twenty-sixth Eldred Wessex had left his Sydney flat ostensibly to purchase a string of pearls to be a birthday present for the woman he had known for a year. A few hours after he had left, Thomas Baker, the ship's steward, had called at the flat asking for him. Less than seventy hours after that call, Baker's nude body was discovered in the Split Point Lighthouse, on the far southern coast of Victoria, only four miles from the homestead where Wessex was born.

What brought Baker to Split Point? If Eldred Wessex, alias Waghorn, had come to the district of his parental home, what had brought him after an absence of ten years? It was reasonable to assume, until Waghorn had been apprehended for questioning, that Eldred Wessex and Thomas Baker had come to Split Point either separately or together. In view of the discovery of the murdered man's effects in the cave, the discovery of the murder weapon in the trunk of Dick Lake, the death of Lake in the effort to retrieve the dead man's effects, it could be assumed that Eldred Wessex had called on his old friend either to assist him in the murder or assist in a plan to defeat justice. For without Eldred Wessex there was no connection between the dead man in the lighthouse and the dead man found at the foot of the cliff.

Wessex, the black rabbit, had probably been in this burrow on or about February twenty-eighth, when Thomas Baker had been shot. Which of these brown rabbits had seen the black one? Which of these brown rabbits had assisted the black rabbit to vanish from the burrow? Or was the black rabbit still within the burrow, lying low like Br'er Rabbit of old?

The stoat entered the burrow entrance at the Inlet Hotel.

The contortive Stug followed him in, and was ordered out by the licensee. There were a couple from a car parked in the driveway, the driver of a delivery van, and Moss Way. Moss nodded a welcome, and called for a drink for Bony, who joined him.

"How's things, Mr. Rawlings?" asked the carrier.

"Very well, Moss. How are you coming along? Found another mate?"

"Not yet," replied Way. "Don't think I will. Manage somehow on me own for a bit. Didn't see you at the funeral."

"No. Had to rush up to Melbourne about my wool. Go off all right?"

"Biggest planting I ever seen. People come for miles. Poor old Dick; never knew how important he was."

"You will certainly miss him," murmured Bony, avoiding a general discussion with people he'd never met.

"Already started," corrected Way. "Loading and unloading on your own's no cop. And living alone ain't no cop, either. Great coffin old Penwarden turned out for Dick. You oughta seen it."

"Oh! Extra special?"

"Yair. Didn't know he had it on hand. Like the one he made for Mrs. Owen, but not with the same polish."

"Red-gum?"

"Same colour."

"Probably the one he was making for me," surmised Bony, and Moss was decidedly interested.

"Yair, that'll be it," he agreed. "Anyhow, the old bloke done her up well. Dick's pals carried the coffin from the truck—our truck—to the graveside, and other pals were the pallbearers. I was one of 'em. Fred Ayling oughta been with us, but The Slide fell down and stopped Alfie reaching him with the news. Alfie had to come back and try another track."

"He and Lake were very firm friends, weren't they?" Bony prompted.

"They were so. Them two and Eldred Wessex were kids together, so Dick told me one time. Dick worried a bit over Eldred Wessex not coming home, and I remember that a few weeks back he was on top of the world, telling me Eldred might be coming home. Nutted out a grand surprise for the old people. Borrowed their car on some excuse and drove to Geelong to pick Eldred up at the train. But Eldred never arrived, and Dick came back without him. Worried him no end for a week or so. Musta worried more'n I thought. Did he seem worried to you?"

"He did not," replied Bony thoughtfully. "Still, he was the kind of man who wouldn't let strangers know what he was thinking. You knew him better than I. Are you sure he was worried?"

"Musta been. I don't reckon he just got up in the middle of a rainy night and went for a walk—not even in his sleep. His old man told Staley Dick usta sleepwalk when he was a kid, and Ma Wessex found him sitting one night on the veranda rail of their house. That was when Dick boarded with her. Usta stop there when he went to school, going home only for week ends and holidays. Fred Ayling usta board there, too. Dick never sleepwalked when he was camping with me."

"When was it that Dick expected Eldred to come home?"

"When! Lemme think." Moss drank deep to aid memory, and Bony asked Washfold to set the drinks up again. "Few weeks back, anyhow!" Way stared at Bony, the frown almost connecting his eyebrows. "I wonder, now. Dick went to meet Eldred a day or so before they found the body in the lighthouse. Think there's——"

"Think nothing," Bony said quickly. "You saw the body in the lighthouse. Everyone did. It wasn't Eldred Wessex."

"I know that, although I've never seen Eldred Wessex. It's funny, though. I——"

"Forget it," Bony snapped. "Dick wasn't the kind of fellow to be mixed up with anything like that."

Slowly, Moss Way nodded agreement.

ABNORMAL REACTIONS

"Ah, good day-ee, Mr. Rawlings, sir!" exclaimed Mr. Penwarden when, on the following day, Bony entered the workshop. "Manner of speaking, though, manner of speaking. Not so good a day to some poor folk. Glad 'e called, though. Telegram came about them blood-woods."

"So! My friend evidently lost no time."

The coffinmaker sat on a case and began to load his pipe. Bony lifted himself to sit on the end of the bench.

"Come from Mildura, that telegram. Just said: 'Logs despatched today to Geelong. Give regards to Bony. Sil Bennet.' That your moniker—Bony?"

Bony winced beneath the failure to notify his friend of his temporary name, and instantly explained that it was a schoolboy nickname. The old man chuckled.

"When I were a young feller the world was remembering another Bony. You don't look like the Frenchy, not by the pictures I seen of him."

"No, I was never handsome," calmly Bony claimed. "When a boy, I was exceptionally thin, and my bones stood out. Hence the appellation. I suppose the railway people will inform you when the logs have reached Geelong?"

"They will so, and I'll send young Moss Way for them. Thank 'e kindly, Mr. Rawlings. That young feller's at a loose end just now. He were talkin' to me yesterday, saying how he missed Dick Lake. Neither thought nothing of that trip over Sweet Fairy Ann. You could all have stopped over there a long time—with a mountain of mullock atop of you and the truck. You been away again?"

"For a couple of days. To Melbourne, you know, to see about my wool. Prices still going up."

"So I read in the paper. Pity you missed the funeral."

"I would rather not have gone." Bony lit a cigarette and carefully bestowed the spent match in the box. "Quite a large number of people attended, I'm told."

"Everyone was there, Mr. Rawlings. Everyone but Fred Ayling and young Alfie Lake who's gone to tell him about Dick. It was a sad day, I assure 'e. Know'd him since he were a baby. I put him in the coffin I was makin' for you, being sure you wouldn't mind. I'll make you another right away. In fact, this board on the bench is to begin her with. Yes, I put him to bunk in the best wood the country has. Glad I were that he wasn't injured about the face. When I'd shaved him and set him to rights, he looked good and comfortable, and could of been sleeping—which, of course, he were."

"His parents were able to attend, of course?"

"Yes. They're blessed with a large family to help 'em take the shock. Little Dick going that way has made me remember more'n usual when him and the other two would race past here and shout out to me, and I'd wave and tell 'em to learn all they could at school. Eli and his old woman were very good to them young rips. Looked after 'em, seen 'em off to school, seen they was fed right to make good bones. She were telling me you went along to have a pitch with Eli. He'd like that.".

"It was a pleasant afternoon," Bony said. "Mr. Wessex claimed my sympathy. To suffer his ailment must be a great trial. Never said outright, you know, but gave me the impression he was bitter about his son not returning home before going off to America. Do you think that young Eldred Wessex really did go to America?"

"Course," came the reply sharply. "Wouldn't have stayed away all this time if he hadn't gone to Amerikee. You seem to doubt it, Mr. Rawlings."

Bony was stubbing his cigarette, and he looked up to meet the clear eyes beneath the mop of white hair.

"Perhaps the thought is father to the wish," he said. "It's a little odd for a young man not to have returned home after those years on active service, but then the younger generation hasn't the consideration for their elders that our generation had. My sympathy has been aroused for both Eli Wessex and his wife, and I find myself a little resentful toward their inconsiderate son."

Penwarden placed his hot pipe on a wall shelf and took up his plane and, with some show of sighting the red-gum board, grumbled agreement with his visitor.

"Eldred was always like that. Wilful, obstinate, selfish. Not the right trainin', Mr. Rawlings, sir. Eldred was the only son. Old Eli was always soft with boys. Not that that is against him, mind you. But he didn't treat his son with balance, and a balanced trainin' is what any boy must have to make a real man of him. Softness should come from the mother; understanding and justice from the father. I often felt soft with my boys, but I never let 'em know it. Eldred would have been worse than he was if it hadn't been for young Ayling."

"Is that so?" encouraged Bony.

"'Tis so, indeed," said the old man, employing the plane. "Fred was a year or two older than Eldred, and Eldred was older than Dick. Always took little Dick's part, always saw to it that Dick had his rightful share of what was going."

"He was, then, the leader?"

"Aye, that he was. Eldred took more notice of him than he did of his father." A deep chuckle came from the full and pink-complexioned face above the halted plane. "Usta fight sometimes, the three of 'em among theirselves, and all together if another lot interfered with 'em."

"I'll warrant this workshop was a magnet for them, Mr. Penwarden."

"You say right, Mr. Rawlings, sir. I mind one day they came in here and Eldred he took up my best finishing plane and tried her on a board with a nail in it. I wouldn't have 'em in for a long time after that. And then, what d'you think? Why, after Eldred left school, he came here to learn my trade. But no good."

"Wouldn't stick at it."

"Wouldn't stick at nothing. Be here getting in my way one day, home helping his father the next day, up in Geelong and workin' at Ford's next week. Got drinkin' too much, and gambling his money away. Went from Ford's to some other place, then back home, then away to Melbourne. And when we tried to talk him into being sensible, he'd only laugh."

"Hopeless, eh?"

"No, not hopeless," asserted the old man. "No young feller's hopeless, rightly handled. Young Eldred was just silly—and artful at the same time. He learned too early and too easy how to put it across his mother. Old Eli saw the way he was going, and he tried to put on the brake, but his wife wouldn't see the way Eldred was takin'. Say anything against Eldred! Eldred could do no wrong. Eldred was the sun of her life, the sun that shone so bright she was blinded. She was harder on Mary. Eldred was always in the right. When he came back that dark night and——"

The plane thudded upon the board, and Bony, who was making a cigarette, glanced up to observe the old man turned from him and visually measuring a sheet of three-ply leaning against the wall. On Penwarden beginning to turn back to the bench, Bony's gaze was directed downward to his fingers.

"When he came back from Ford's and told his mother he would never work else but on the farm, she believed him."

"Well, well," Bony said, lighting the cigarette. "Most women are soft with their sons." There was a telltale flush on the old man's face and a mask before the bright blue eyes, and not to permit suspicion that the slip had been noted, Bony went on: "Like many another wild young man, no doubt Eldred will settle down sometime. Better to sow the wild oats in the twenties than the forties."

"You say true, Mr. Rawlings, sir, you say true," and Bony detected a note of relief. The switch of subjects seemed to confirm it. "This here board is for your coffin. I had t'others all put together time the news about Dick came. So I chose this 'un, and a few more to build yours. Ought to be ready for a fitting in a couple of days."

"It's very good of you, Mr. Penwarden."

"Good for good, Mr. Rawlings. Them bloodwoods have been in my mind as much as a fine dress in the mind of a young gal to be married. You know, wood's wood. I mind me many a year ago I were down on the beach and found a tough plank the like of which I'd never seen. I made the mantel in our sitting room out of her. Daffodil yellow she be, and no one can tell me the name of the tree. Musta come a long way in the sea. A university man looked at her and he said she never come from an Australian tree. Yes, wood's wood. This here casket of yours will have the best red gum, and very extra polishin'. You're going to remember old Ed Penwarden every time you look at her."

"I'm sure to."

The plane was taken up and the blade was scrutinised and reset. Dropping the implement on the board was not normal to this craftsman to whom tools were extremely precious. The plane was again put to work, and a moment later a step sounded just beyond the wide door.

Bony turned to see Fred Ayling enter. Old Penwarden put down his plane. Ayling came forward, striding over the shavings-littered floor as though on a mission of dramatic import.

"Good day, Ed!" And to Bony: "Day!"

"Same to you, Fred!" chirped the old man. "Glad to be lookin' at you."

"An' me you, Ed." Ayling stood firmly balanced on his feet. His heavy brows were low to the dark eyes, and the eyes were small. "Thanks for doing a good job with Dick's box. His old man was telling me about it. What's it going to cost? I want to pay for it."

"I ain't worked her out yet, Fred. By and by, perhaps. You have much trouble getting across The Slide?"

"You could work out the cost now, couldn't you?" persisted the axeman. "Dick and me were cobbers. You know that. I want to do something for Dick."

Penwarden took down his pipe and fingered it. He appeared to ponder, and Ayling gave him half a minute.

"You work out the cost right now, and I'll square the account."

"Well, I don't know about that, Fred. You see, I was thinkin' of making her a kind of present to poor Dick, havin' know'd him since he were a baby and smacked his bottom and boxed his ears more'n once for cheekin' me."

Ayling was insistent. His face was grim, and it seemed that the paramount emotion ruling him was anger, not grief.

"I want to pay, and I'm going to pay," he announced slowly. "He was my cobber, not yours, Ed. You tot it up right now. How much?"

"Ha, well! I suppose if you want to you want to." The old man returned the pipe to the shelf and put on a pair of steel-rimmed glasses. From a wall nail he lifted down a child's school slate, cleaned it with spit and rag, and proceeded to draw figures. Ayling remained motionless, keeping his gaze directed to the coffinmaker. The silence was oppressive.

"Here she be, Fred," came the old man's soft voice. "Material and labour brings her up to twenty-five pound and ten shillings."

Ayling produced a wallet and counted the money in notes upon the bench, and it was so quiet that Bony heard the rustle of the paper.

"Send us a receipt sometime, Ed," Ayling said, stepping backward from the bench until Penwarden and Bony were to his front. His eyes were again small and his voice clipped when he spoke to Bony.

"Funny thing you happened to be down at the beach that morning to find Dick dead and all broken up."

"Chance," Bony said. "The sea was raging that morning and I wanted to look at it. What is peculiar about my being there?"

"That all you found—the body?"

"Should I have found anything beside the body?"

"Don't know. You wouldn't be putting anything over?"

"I don't understand you," Bony countered.

"And I don't understand you, Mister Rawlings. I may—one day. One day I may get to know why you're nosing around down here—walking the roads after dark, asking questions about things and people what don't concern any visitor. There's some——"

"That'll be enough from you, Fred, my boy," interposed the old man. "You clear off and think things over, and give yourself a chance to calm down. Poor Dick's death don't only affect you, you know. He was your cobber, as you say. And he was my friend, same as you and Mr. Rawlings. I'll have no ill words spoken in my workshop."

Without countering that firmly spoken declaration, Fred Ayling strode to the door and passed from sight, and again the old man took down his pipe and stood merely fingering it. It became obvious that he waited for Ayling to withdraw from earshot.

"That's Fred," presently he said. "That's Fred as he allus was. Good feller, and straight. Hot-tempered, generous, patient, true. Him and Dick were allus good cobbers. Don't be put out, Mr. Rawlings, sir. Fred'll be good again tomorrow."

"Without doubt," agreed Bony. "Naturally he's very upset, and probably made more so having been unable to be at the funeral. It was good of you to concede him the privilege of paying for the casket."

" 'Tain't nuthin'." The old man struck a match and lit his pipe to his satisfaction before adding: "When you gets old you learns wisdom how to deal with others." A smile crept into the bright blue eyes. "I've learned when to give way, and how much. Don't you say nuthin' to no one, Mr. Rawlings, sir, but that coffin Dick Lake's sleepin' in is worth a hundred pounds of anyone's money."

DEAD MAN'S TRACKS

There was neither a break in the leaden sky nor a mark on the leaden sea, save where it surged against the claws of Split Point. The air was still and cold.

Amid the tea tree on the headland was a bower overlooking the ocean, and there Bony sat on a magazine and Stug uneasily squatted at his side. Together they had been tramping about the cliffs, and the dog had chased rabbits that had tossed their heels and defied him. Both man and dog had collected many burrs.

The problem occupying Bony's mind was whether the time was come to declare himself and question in an official capacity. Earlier this day he had driven to Lorne, where he had spoken with the Superintendent by telephone and had learned that Waghorn had not been seen by Sydney's underworld for many weeks and that he had not been picked up by the police in any capital city.

Failure to find Waghorn irritated Bolt, and gave Bony satisfaction by strengthening conviction that Eldred Wessex had come to Split Point prior to the discovery of the body in the lighthouse.

Moss Way had said that Lake went to Geelong to meet Eldred off the train and had returned without him. Old Penwarden had inadvertently let slip the half statement that Eldred had come home "that dark night." The night of February twenty-eighth–March first was a dark night. The slip had confused the old man, of that there was no doubt.

"Yes, yes, Stug! Relax," Bony urged the dog. "Leave my sock alone."

What kind of a man was he who breakfasted with Jean Stebbings on the morning of her birthday, then walked out of the flat and never returned? Why, the latest edition of the youth who tried to work for Penwarden, attempted to help his father, dallied awhile at the Ford Motor Works and elsewhere. He was impetuous, rash, restless, a liar, conceited, able to put forward a pseudo charm, ruthless and cold and imaginative. He conformed to a type as easily recognisable as that of Dick Lake.

"I shall have to tackle Moss Way with greater determination," Bony said to the dog, and Stug continued to worry a sock and, with teeth bared, delicately detached from the wool one of several burrs. "I must find out if Lake mentioned another man he expected to accompany Eldred Wessex. Perhaps, in view of all the circumstances, Baker did accompany Eldred, and Dick Lake did meet them at the station and drive them to Split Point. Oh well, Stug! As Penwarden would say: 'Good for good.' I now see that you want me to relieve you of a few uncomfortable burrs in exchange for the service you are doing me."

Pulling burrs from the dog's hair produced plain gratitude that the uneasiness had at last been understood, and Stug determinedly proceeded to bite away the remaining burrs clinging to socks and trouser cuffs.

"I don't think you know Eldred Wessex," Bony said. "So what, Stug? Dick Lake must have gone to Geelong on February twenty-seventh or twenty-eighth and met Eldred, who either flew down to Melbourne or caught the night express. From Melbourne to Geelong by train would be only a little more than an hour. I can see Lake meeting his pal. But I cannot see how Baker entered the picture where he remained as a naked corpse.

"The money found in the wallet assumed to have belonged to the dead man is a point which I find of greatest interest," Bony confessed to the dog. "All told, the amount was £89.7.5. As the novelists would say, it is out of character for Eldred Wessex to have left that money with the dead man's clothes. I am strongly inclined to think it would be entirely in character for Dick Lake to have left money and wallet, even taking care to place the odd seven and fivepence inside the wallet. That indicates a strong sense of honesty in Lake. Why the revolver was not left in the cave would indicate that it belonged not to the dead man but either to Eldred or Lake. . . .

"Well, Lake is now beyond the reach of the stoat, but Wessex isn't. Eldred Wessex is still at large, living possibly somewhere on his father's farm, probably over beyond Sweet Fairy Ann with or near Fred Ayling. I anticipated that Bolt would fail to find him as

Waghorn, which is why I gave the Super that little something to occupy his attention. And now, Stug, as Pepys would say: 'Home for a glass of ale and a rousing good dinner.' Many thanks for divesting me of those burrs."

Stug staggered down the headland slope behind Bony, and he lurched up the highway to the Inlet Hotel as though nothing mattered save to flop upon the mat outside the barroom door. Yet, with spasmodic enthusiasm, he accompanied Bony down the road after dinner, and along the inlet track to the camp where Moss Way lived.

It was a one-room iron shack set back off the road between Penwarden's house and his workshop, and Moss was found seated on a case at a rough deal table and reading a newspaper by the aid of a storm lantern.

"Picking winners?" Bony surmised from the doorway.

"Hullo, Mr. Rawlings! Come in! Matter of fact, I was."

There were two rough bunks, one either side the open hearth. Cooking utensils, food wrapped in paper, bottled condiments, created the confusion seemingly inseparable from men baching for themselves. Moss indicated a broken chair beside the fire and moved his case to sit with the visitor. Stug silently came in and lay down at Bony's feet.

"How you been puttin' in the day?" asked Moss.

"Went to Lorne this morning. Tramped along the cliffs this afternoon. Calm sea. Seems too cold for rain."

"Might blow a dry easterly tomorrow. Glass at the pub's high."

No anxiety in the easy voice. Despite the chill of the night, Moss sat in his cotton vest, in sharp contrast with the heavy working trousers and nail-studded boots.

"You will have to find another partner," Bony said, lighting a cigarette.

"Yair," agreed the long man. "Put it on Fred Ayling last night. Must have been the wrong time. Fred was terrible sore about something. He came in to see if there was anything left of Dick's. I asked him what about it, and he said he might be goin' to work for Ma Wessex."

"What d'you think he was sore about?"

"Aw, I don't know. Always was a moody bloke. Been living alone too long, I suppose."

The dog raised his head and growled—and went off to sleep. Bony steered the conversation away from Ayling to the safer waters near the ports of General Subjects. It was fully half an hour before he steered it back to the point he wished to anchor it.

"You'd think that Eldred Wessex would have made certain of being at Dick's funeral, wouldn't you?" he suggested.

"Yes . . . and no, from what I've heard of Eldred Wessex," replied Moss. "Don't know much about him, not being one of the mob around here. You're either in or you're out, and if you are out you don't never get in, if you know what I mean. What I reckon is that Eldred never was any good, but he was able to put it over people, especially his friends. Use 'em up, right and left, and never blink an eyelid."

"Couldn't have bothered much about writing to Dick explaining why he didn't arrive at Geelong."

"That's what worried Dick, I think. And Dick waiting all that day, and, when Eldred didn't come off the train, camping in the car all night outside the station, and waiting all the next day too."

"A long wait," murmured Bony.

"You're telling me. He left here at one to meet the two-twenty in from Melbourne. All keyed up, too. Got a telegram early that morning, and we drove out to Eli's place to borrow the car, Dick putting up a tale he wanted to meet a girl friend for the day. He aimed to bring Eldred back on the quiet and walk in on the old people to give 'em the surprise of their sweet lives. I come across that telegram this morning. Found it stuck behind the flour tin up there."

"H'm!" murmured Bony, rubbing his nose with a finger tip to prevent Moss from noting how the nostrils quivered.

"Dick musta put it there and then forgot all about it," Moss went on. "Terrible disappointed when he came home, he was. I come in for a drink of tea and some grub about midday, and there's Dick cleaning up his best clothes. With his other clothes he wouldn't care a damn if the backside of his pants was hanging down and trailing after him. His best clothes, though, they had to be looked after like he was getting married. I'll get that telegram. You take a deck at it."

Moss obtained the flimsy from a writing pad.

"Shows how artful Eldred was to beat the Post Office," he said, passing the message to Bony.

It was accepted by the G.P.O., Sydney, at 5.35 P.M., February 26, and read:

HOPE TO ARRIVE GEELONG PER TRAIN ABOUT TWO TOMORROW. WANT YOU MEET ME WITH CAR. SAY NOTHING TO ANYONE, AS FATHER MIGHT GET TO HEAR ABOUT US.

LOVE ALWAYS.
ETHEL

"Ethel!" purred Bony, and Stug growled without lifting his muzzle from his paws.

"Eldred," Moss said triumphantly. "Dick didn't know any Ethel. Told me he didn't, anyhow. Said the telegram was from Eldred."

"He could have come home for the funeral," Bony persisted. "Probably his failure to do so upset Fred Ayling."

"Musta. Fred told me to keep out of it and not to talk about Dick. As though Dick belonged to him. I've been Dick's cobber and partner since he came back from the war, and I'm going to talk as much as I like. There's some things, though, that I'm not going to talk about. Wouldn't have talked about 'em to you, only you're a sort of friend, going over Sweet Fairy Ann with us, and Dick saying you was all right. What's in my mind, did Dick spend that night in Geelong?"

"What's the point?" objected Bony.

"I dunno. Washfold went to Anglesea that evening, and he thought he saw Wessex' car parked beside the road at the Memorial Lookout."

"That's on a hill this side of Anglesea, isn't it?"

"Yes. I never said nothing to Washfold about Dick going to Geelong, and what time he said he came home. Nothing to do with Bert Washfold."

"No, of course not. Better forgotten, eh?"

Moss stared hard at Bony and nodded.

A few minutes after that Bony left, and at ten o'clock the following morning he was seated in Bolt's car, parked outside the Geelong Railway Station, and watching the passengers coming off the first train from the city. There, following a telephoned request, a detective attached to Divisional Headquarters joined him.

"Yes, I'm Inspector Bonaparte. Get in the car. What is the C.I.B.'s report?"

"That at 9 A.M. this morning Waghorn had not been located, sir," replied the detective crisply. He was a slight, grey-eyed man whose chief distinction was not to look like a policeman.

"You were on the lighthouse murder investigation?"

"Yes, sir. I know the district and the people. Was stationed at Lorne for seven years in uniform."

"You know, then, the people living behind the inlet—the Wessexes, the Lakes, and the Owens?"

"Yes, sir. More than once I had to visit the Wessex farm about the son. Before the war that was. Eldred just missed being charged twice in the period 1936–39. He made the old people sick worrying about him. Same old setup, sir. Doting mother and weak father."

"And Richard Lake, recently found dead at the foot of Split Point?"

"Bit of a lad, but nothing bad to him. Pity he ended like that. Did well in the Army, I understand."

"What of Lake's partner?"

"Moss Way! Nothing against him. Steady sort of chap."

"And Fred Ayling?"

"Slightly erratic. Know nothing to his disadvantage, sir."

"H'm! Most helpful that you know all these people. Smoke if you want to, whilst I explain what I want done. Bear in mind the date that Fisher found the body in the wall locker. On February twenty-seventh, at about two o'clock in the afternoon, Dick Lake came here and parked Eli Wessex' car to wait for a man coming off the two-twenty train from Melbourne.

"Lake was wearing his best suit, which is important. The friend did not arrive by that train. It is thought that he did not arrive until the next day, and that Lake camped in the car throughout the night of February twenty-seventh to twenty-eighth. It is thought the friend accompanied Lake to Split Point. The friend could have been accompanied by a friend—another important point.

"As you are known to every publican in Geelong, I want Lake tracked after he arrived at this place. Doubtless he would eat at the café he used when coming here with Moss Way to deliver and call for goods. Doubtless he had his favourite hotels between here and the exit from Geelong. I want to know when Lake left Geelong, and whether he was accompanied by one or two men. And, if possible, the description of them. You can take this car. I will wait hereabouts for you."

"Very well, sir."

The detective drove away, and Bony bought a morning paper and sought a quiet café for tea and sandwiches. When at noon the Geelong detective had not returned, he telephoned Bolt.

"Still falling down on the old job?" he asked pleasantly.

"You will never know until *you* do," growled the vast man from his comfortable office. "What goes, Bony?"

Bony explained that he had called on the Geelong police for the services of a detective, saying:

"When that plain-clothes man reports to his superior officer, they are going to be interested and might interfere more than I want. You order them to leave my work to me."

"Yes, sir," snarled Bolt. "What the hell are you doing in Geelong?"

"Tracking a dead man," serenely replied Bony. "But I still want Waghorn—hat, boots, and all. I know you promised him to me, Super, but I am somewhat impatient."

"Must be ill or something—to be impatient, Bony. All right, blast you! I'll fix it with the officer down there. Don't you go getting into trouble, now. Your Chief's been talking over trunk line with my Chief. Wants to know why the hell you're taking such a long time to wind up a simple little murder case. Says that a real policeman would have *finalised* the job weeks ago."

"As well for you—and the law—that I'm not a real policeman," snapped Bony, and cut the connection.

The Geelong detective didn't turn up until after three o'clock.

"Found a clear trail at the Belmont Hotel, sir," he reported. "The men, Lake and Way, are well known there both to the licensee and his barman. As you know, it's the last hotel out of Geelong on the road to Split Point.

"The barman remembers that Lake called there one afternoon at about the time of the lighthouse murder, and he remembers because it was the first and only time he saw Lake wearing a good suit. The exact date he can't fix, but he says it was raining hard and steady that afternoon. It was the afternoon of February twenty-eighth, because it didn't rain on February twenty-seventh, or on March first, second, or third.

"The barman couldn't remember if Lake was accompanied, meaning that he was alone when he entered the bar. However, in the bar were three men who knew Lake, and the barman was able to give me their names and addresses.

"I interviewed the three men. They remember drinking with Lake that afternoon. They are agreed that he entered the bar alone and also that he bought a bottle of brandy which he put into a pocket of his overcoat. They are also agreed that Lake did not take more than four small glasses of beer, which to them was strange, as they had never known him to drink small beers.

"One of the three could tell more than the others. They wanted Lake to stay drinking with them, but he said he'd have to keep sober as he had a girl friend out in the car. One man followed him outside the bar, continuing to urge him to have a last drink for the road. He says that inside the car, in the back seat, were two people. One of them he thinks was a man, and the other could have been a woman. He can't be sure, as the side-curtain window was yellow and dirty. He watched Lake drive off along the road to Anglesea and Split Point."

Bony said nothing for a full minute, and then to thank the detective for a good job of work.

He had hoped for a sprat and had been given a whale.

ED PENWARDEN'S MISTAKE

Three men had left the Belmont Hotel for Split Point, for Bony could not accept the view that one of Dick Lake's passengers was a woman. Lake was dead. His companions had been careful to avoid recognition by remaining in the back seat of the car, and of those two, Eldred Wessex was surely one. The other was dead, were he Thomas Baker.

The clue of the red-gum shaving found in the lighthouse had produced a result, although a scent rather than a fingerprint. Elimination had reduced the possible agents of conveyance from the carpenter's workshop to the lighthouse to one of three men: the murderer, the murderer's accomplice, the victim. Now the victim could be discarded, and there remained the two agents named, viz.: Dick Lake and Eldred Wessex.

Either one or both had been inside Penwarden's workshop immediately before the nude body was entombed in the lighthouse wall. And old Penwarden knew it.

How to tackle the coffinmaker? With the sharp scalpel of the expert investigator, or with the soft and soothing blah of the diplomat? Bony chose the alternative.

The day was sunny and warm for the month of May, and after lunch he strolled with Stug down the curve of the highway, and so to the building where laboured the master craftsman.

"Hullo, Mr. Rawlings, sir!" greeted the old man. "Come on in and sit you down and gas." A throaty chuckle. "My old woman's allus on to me for gassin'. Says I do nothing else the livelong day. Gas, gas, gas, and she workin' her fingers to the bone. You ever seen your wife's finger bones?"

"They are too well padded," replied Bony, occupying his favorite end of the bench. "Any further word about the bloodwood logs?"

"Not yet. The railways take their time these days. Could be a full week, even two, afore them logs arrive in Geelong." The work-hardened fingers combed back the long white hair, and the blue eyes beamed. "Tell you what, Mr. Rawlings. I'll make and polish a shelf for your sitting room. Scarlet she'll be, with the shine to her like my daffodil yellow one. You come in for a cup of tea with me and the old woman afore you leave Split Point—just to look at that bit of flotsam."

"Thank you. I'd like to."

"Your holiday got much more to go?"

"Perhaps another week."

The old man took up a rule and measured a rough length of scantling. He jotted figures on the slate, pondered on them, and, having pencilled a mark on the wood and sawn along it, he straightened and regarded Bony with eyes narrowed by the broad smile.

"I've assembled her," he said. "Put her together this morning. No polishing, mind. Still see the joints. Like to look at her?"

"Of course," replied Bony, slipping off the bench.

"Takes a time to put the gloss on her," went on Penwarden. "I likes to put in an hour or two every day for a week, and then give her a rest for a week or so. You know, wood's wood. When a man dies, he rots. When a tree dies, 'specially them red gums, she never rots—leastways not for centuries. The sap dries out after she dies, but the wood keeps a sort of spirit that goes on for years and years.

"You have to love the wood, and coax it, and talk to it while you polishes and polishes, and after a bit, if you listen hard enough, you'll hear the wood talkin' to you like a cat when she's stroked. You seen the coffin I made for Mrs. Owen. I'll make yours to look as good, and, centuries to come, me and you will still be lying snug. I got her in the parlour."

Having by now conquered the superstitious dread of coffins, and able calmly to regard objectively Mr. Penwarden's creations, Bony followed the ancient to the "parlor" with pleasurable anticipation.

"Here she be!" cried the old man when they stood either side the dull red casket on the trestles. "Here she be in the makin'. The unpolished gem, the smoulderin' fire, the untested character."

He raised the lid on its hidden hinges, and the lid remained in its balanced upright position, and he regarded Bony with eyes lit by pride and undimmed by the decades. Bony felt the satin smoothness of the wood, was reminded of the red sand of the inland, the real heart of Australia which fools continue to claim is dead. He lowered the lid and heard the air compression, so perfect was its fit.

"You should be very proud of your work," he said. "Wrong word, for which I'm sorry. Art is the word, for you are indeed an artist."

"Nay, Mr. Rawlings, sir. A good tradesman, that's all. I've lived a long time in the one abiding place, but I've learned much and Time has done a bit of polishin' to me too. This here job is good, I'll say that for it, and all that's needed is to work on her and coax her to show us the glory of her heart. Now just you take a fittin' to make sure you lies comfortable, and then when you get her home you pushes her under the bed and don't think of her . . . only now and then. We all want a corrector, Mr. Rawlings, sir, and there's nothin' like the sight of a coffin to melt away pride and vanity. Now let's take that fitting."

"You want me to lie down in it?"

"Just to make sure she's right to take the small of your back, and the fit of your neck. No need to take your shoes off. They won't do no damage."

"Very well," assented Bony. The old man, had he a beard, could be Father Time, and the rule he waved in his left hand the scythe.

Bony settled himself, and Penwarden placed his legs straight and his feet together. All that could be seen of him by Bony was the upper third of his body.

"Ah!" breathed the craftsman. "My guess of your length was true. Now how does your neck and head rest? Just you say. We'll make sure she's nice and easy."

"A little could be taken off the curve of the neck rest," Bony decided, and sat up to indicate a point where the carved rest pressed too sharply.

"That's so!" exclaimed the old man. "About a shavin' or two will fix that. Down you go, and we'll make sure of your back."

"The back seems to be all right," Bony said, moving his body and relaxing. "Yes, quite good. There's no doubt"—the broken sentence was completed before his mind registered the slam of the lid—"you are a good tradesman."

Accident, of course! He expected the lid to be raised instantly, and when it was not, he lifted his hands to press it upward. He was able to raise it—a fraction of an inch.

"Mr. Penwarden!" he called, and used his knees to assist his hands. The lid could not be raised higher than that fraction of one inch. "Mr. Penwarden! Raise the lid!"

Leg and arm muscles relaxed and the lid sank, the air being compressed like escaping steam. The blackness of the grave, and confines of the grave, encompassed him. A great shout pounded in his ears, and he realised it was his own voice. With all his strength he pushed upward—and forced up the lid that fraction of an inch.

"Penwarden!" he shouted. "Penwarden, let me out! This is beyond a joke. D'you hear? Let me out at once."

"Ah, Mr. Rawlings, sir. 'Tis indeed beyond a joke."

The voice was far distant and yet blared in his right ear. He maintained the upward pressure of the lid and heard the scrape of the small wedge. His mind was cool, but his body trembled violently. Again the voice spoke into his ear.

"As we just agreed, this is not a joke."

"Then let me out, Mr. Penwarden," cried Bony, and was mortified by the note of fear in his own voice.

"You see, Mr. Rawlings, sir, it's like this," went on the old man without. "I took you for a visitor to Split Point, a pleasant gentleman taking a holiday. I sort of took to you, and liked to do a bit of gassin' with you. But you're not what you make out. You came to Split Point to make more trouble for them who's been troubled more'n enough. What's done was done, and what's past is past, but you, Mr. Rawlings, intends adding trouble to trouble and grief to grief."

"What the devil do you mean?" demanded Bony, knowing that the only escape was via his tongue.

"Evildoers tread in the steps of evildoers. You are an octopus that crawls from the sea to trap good clean life in God's own world. I am going to leave you for a little while, Mr. Rawlings, sir, just for a little while. I'll leave the lid wedged so's you will get air and take the opportunity to make your peace with the Eternal. You won't raise the lid any more, because she's set fast. And no one will hear your shoutin', exceptin' the Eternal."

"What are you driving at?" shouted Bony. "I've done you no injury. Release me at once."

"We know all about the man in the wall of the lighthouse, Mr. Rawlings, sir. We know what he did to Eldred Wessex, and what Eldred did to him. We know you came here to find out what happened to that man and who killed him, that you can blackmail poor Eldred's parents into telling you where he is."

Bony continued to expostulate, conscious of the note of desperation in his voice.

"We know," continued Penwarden, "we know you went to the cave under the cliff, and found what you found. You came here to blackmail Eldred's father and mother. And no mercy on them. And no mercy on you. You shall die in your coffin and be buried evermore."

There was no exultancy in the ancient's voice, no hint of an unbalanced mind. The voice was hard, the enunciation distinct. The voice was without heat, implacable. Fighting for control, Bony said:

"Now you listen to me, Mr. Penwarden. I am not an associate of the man found dead in the lighthouse. I am a police officer, investigating the murder of the man who is known as Thomas Baker. I am Detective Inspector Napoleon Bonaparte. You must remember that my friend who sent you the telegram saying he'd despatched the bloodwood logs also said for you to remember him to his friend Bony."

The echo of his voice within the coffin dwindled into the fetid twilight. The silence was unbroken, and Bony thought the old man had gone away. He said rapidly, however:

"I know that Dick Lake was in that crime. Constable Staley and I found the revolver in Dick's trunk at his camp, the weapon which killed Baker. The experts at Police Headquarters have examined it, and the bullet found in the body has the marks on it made by the barrel. If you kill me, Penwarden, other policemen will come to search for me. They will carry on where I left off. They will inform Dick's parents about that revolver and say that Dick shot Thomas Baker. You can't stop it, Mr. Penwarden. You can't stop justice once it begins working."

Again that withdrawal of sound into the twilight. Again the

dreadful silence. This time the silence was ended by a plaintive cry. The lid was lifted. Daylight rushed upon Bony, and the sweet aroma of wood shavings swept like brooms through the corridors of his haunted mind. Arms slid under him, lifted him, assisted him up and out of the coffin. His legs were almost paralysed, and his breathing was stertorous. Old arms, strong yet, and made stronger still by emotion, helped him to the wall, there to let him down with his back resting.

Old Penwarden fell to his knees before Bony, his hands upon the floor. Horror lived in his blue eyes, matching the horror still living in the blue eyes of Napoleon Bonaparte. His voice was like the wind in bulrushes.

"Mr. Rawlings, sir! Mr.—Inspector Bonaparte, sir—Mr. Rawlings! I didn't know. I made a mistake, 'deed I did. Take your time, Mr. Rawlings, sir. Just you take your time."

THE MASTERMIND

It was Bony who first recovered. He assisted Penwarden to his feet, felt the trembling of the old body, was perturbed by the prospect of heart failure cutting off a vital source of information.

"We'll go out to the workshop and talk about it," he said, finding it necessary to steer the old man to the packing case at the bench. Having sat him down, Bony took from the wall shelf the pipe and the tin of tobacco and lifted himself to sit on the bench. With effort to control his fingers, he rolled a cigarette.

"Be easy, Mr. Penwarden," he urged the old man, who sat with face turned down to the hands resting on his knees. "I am, indeed, a detective inspector investigating the death of the man in the lighthouse, and it seems that you have had the idea that I was a bird of entirely different plumage."

"That's how 'twas, Mr. Rawlings, sir." Penwarden reached for pipe and tobacco, and the hand trembled violently. "I am truly sorry I was so mistaken, and very glad that the mistake didn't end in a bad way . . . for both of us. What will you be doing about it?"

"Having admitted the mistake, and the mistake not having ended in a bad way, nothing. We will forget about that little episode and concentrate on matters of greater importance. Now light your pipe and be easy. As you urged me to do, take your time."

"That be very kind of you, Mr. Rawlings, sir. What I done was in thinkin' for others. Now I can see what an old fool I was. Ah me! 'Tis a sad thing that the Lord thrashes those He loves, and if you would spare 'em all you can, I'm sure your reward in the hereafter would be certain."

"If you refer to the innocent, Mr. Penwarden, I have known many instances when the police have striven to lessen the suffering of innocent persons occasioned by the guilty," Bony said quietly. "After all, we policemen are ordinary men. We are fathers and sons or brothers. We uphold the law, and try to do so impersonally, and the older we become, so are we the more inclined to be sympathetic, even to the criminal, who is, of course, suffering an illness of the mind."

Penwarden puffed vigorously at his pipe without speaking, till he put the pipe down on the bench and heaved a sigh. The unwrinkled face was gaining a little of its normal pinkness, and the hands were less agitated. Bony waited patiently, his mind sponged clean of rancour, and presently the old man spoke.

"It were Fred Ayling who told me about you finding their old cave, and then telling me you must be a friend of the man they found dead in the lighthouse. That man had Eldred Wessex in his clutches. Fred warned me against you, and I sharpened my wits and put two and two together. I happened to see you going into Moss Way's camp t'other night, and I sneaked close and heard him and you talking. You played him well, and I come to be sure about you. Now I'm sad at heart, Mr. Rawlings, sir, that I gave you such a fright.

"I'll have to go back a long way to the time I came here as a lad with nothing but the strength in me arms and back. In them days Eli Wessex was a mere boy, and Tom Owen wasn't born. No one hereabout had much money, and to journey to Melbourne was a big thing to do.

"In course of time we all took wives and sired children, and we never had no quarrels like most neighbours have. When the present Lake's father and mother came to take up land, we helped 'em to their feet. When the fires came and burned the Owens out, we set 'em up again. When the present Lake broke his leg, Tom Owen bossed the lads and seen to it they did their work. All of us did our best to be upright and God-fearing.

"It were Eli Wessex' father who set me up as wheelwright and undertaker. He advanced me a hundred pounds, and when I was able to repay the debt he was dead, and Eli wouldn't take the money . . . wiped out the debt, sayin' I'd already paid it in service.

"My sons grew up before Eldred, and Dick Lake and Fred Ayling, and it was Eli who had 'em over to his place and read and talked to 'em and set their feet firmly on the road. To this day my sons haven't forgot Eli, and what Eli did for 'em."

"Then came up Eldred, with Dick and Fred, and Eli did for them what he did for my boys. Boys are boys, and the generations don't change 'em. There's no difference between boys and young horses. They likes to show off. They wants to be men before their whiskers sprout, and when their whiskers do grow long enough to shave off, most of 'em quiet down and get a bit of sense. My sons did. So did Dick Lake, in his own way, and Fred Ayling in his.

"But Eldred, he never got sense, never got past the showing-off stage, never took in anything from his father. Several times before the war a policeman came to find where Eldred was, and to tell Eli and his wife that if they didn't put a brake on him he'd find himself in gaol. All of us thought that the Army would tame him.

"He never went to America after the war. He never came home, neither. Said he was trying to make good before he came home. I know he didn't make good, 'cos he wrote asking me for money, and saying I was not to tell his parents about it.

"I sent him the money to Sydney. It was a fairish bit, too. A couple of months after that he wrote for more, and more I sent him, thinking about that hundred pounds I never repaid his grandfather. When he wrote for the third time asking for money, I refused him. It was only the other day that I learned that his mother used to send him money, and even Dick Lake did.

"And then one morning Dick Lake popped in here to tell me that

Eldred was coming home. He'd had a telegram from Eldred sayin' he'd be arriving at Geelong that very day, and Dick planned to meet him and take him home to give Eli and his wife the surprise of their lives. Dick borrowed Eli's car and went up to Geelong, but he didn't come back that day, or the next day till ten that night.

"He knocked on my front door, and I answered, as the old woman had gone to bed. Dick tells me he wants to talk private like, and would I go with him to the workshop. We came here, me carrying a hurricane lamp. I set the lamp down here on this here bench, and Dick's beside me. Then I hears a noise behind me, and I turns round to see Eldred.

"He's the same Eldred, yet different. Older, of course. There's no colour to his face. His mouth is sort of saggin' and both cheeks are twitching like he's got the palsy. I looks at him, and he looks at me, and we don't say a word. Dick says:

"'Me and Eldred is up against it, Ed. Want to talk it over, sort of, like when we were kids. Pretty serious this time, though. Eldred's all played out, and I can't think straight. It's terrible crook, Ed!'

"Dick wasn't cocky, like usual. He looked like he did when he was a little feller and come to me to get him out of scrapes. He made me fear, and Eldred stood there slobberin' and saying something over and over what I couldn't understand. Him I didn't care tuppence for. I went over to the door and locked it. Then I came back to the bench and put the light out, so's no one would know we were here, and I told Dick to fess up."

Penwarden lit his pipe with hands which trembled as much as when he had assisted Bony from the coffin. The pipe gave no ease to the memory of that night, and again he discarded it.

"Eldred got off the train at Geelong in the late afternoon after Dick's been waiting outside the station since the day before. Dick seen him leaving the station and went to meet him. Eldred's a bit nervous of something, and he wants to know this and that, and Dick tells him he had Eli's car parked opposite. They get into the car, and then, just before they can get away, a stranger to Dick comes up and says: 'I'm going with Eldred! Little spot of business to settle.'

"Dick looks at Eldred and Eldred nods all right, and the stranger

172

gets into the back seat with Eldred. They don't talk, and Dick drives through the town and when he comes to the Belmont Hotel he stops there for a drink. The others won't leave the car, and Eldred don't want Dick to go into the pub, but Dick is a bit sore by this time and he has his way. After a bit, he bought a bottle of brandy and went out to the car. Dick gets in and drives on for Split Point.

"All the way to Anglesea, Eldred and the stranger in the back don't speak a word, and when they get to the top of the hill by the Memorial, Dick pulls off the road and parks, and he says he don't go no further until he hears what's what.

"It's getting dark by this time, and 'cos Dick hasn't had nothin' to eat since breakfast, he oughtn't to have opened that brandy bottle. The bottle goes the round, and then Eldred says that the stranger thinks he's got a holt on him. The stranger says he's certainly got a good holt on Eldred, and that if he don't part up with something over four hundred pounds owing to him, he'll see Eldred's father about it. Then he tells Dick how Eldred's been in business with him, selling drugs and smuggled pearls and suchlike, and had cleared off from Sydney thinking he'd escape paying the stranger his share.

"There's quite an argument up there by the Memorial. Eldred don't deny anything, and the stranger tells of other things about Eldred worse'n peddling cocaine. Dick says 'tis best to take 'em both back to Geelong, for he don't want either of 'em, let alone both, walking in on Eli and his wife. But the stranger won't hear of that. Says nothing will stop him talking to Eldred's father, exceptin' four hundred and some pounds.

"The argument gets hot and hotter, and presently Eldred tells the stranger that if he don't get out of the car, he'll bash him. So the stranger leaves, and Eldred gets out too. Then Eldred punches the stranger and knocks him down. Dick can see him lying in the faint light from the rear lamp, and he can see most of Eldred too. And as the stranger's lying on his back, Eldred shoots him.

"Dick's out like a flash. In time to stop Eldred firing again. He wrestles for the gun and takes it off Eldred, and when he bends down over the stranger he knows murder has been done. They sit on the running board, with the dead man at their feet. Eldred is crying

173

and Dick don't know what to do. He's thinkin' of Eli and Eldred's mother. And he's still thinkin' of them when he fesses up to me.

"In the dark we sit here for a long time," continued old Penwarden. "Mostly it's silent, sometimes Dick askin' me what to do, sometimes Eldred whining it wasn't his fault, that he didn't mean to shoot. And me just thinkin' what's best to do.

"Even now you've got me to rights, Mr. Rawlings, sir, I'm not fretful over what I advised Dick to do. There's Eldred, a no-good waster, a be-devilled human who's never given anything but sorrow. There's the stranger, another waster, a defier of the law, a despoiler of souls with his evil drugs. There's Eli, well-nigh helpless, sittin' and lyin' and just thinkin' and being troubled like Job. And there's his wife who never spared herself, who poured out a mighty love upon her only man-child. They mustn't know about murder. And there's only Dick Lake and me to stop 'em from knowing.

"What use to tell Eldred he ought'n to have done it? What use to say anything to Eldred? Eldred's finished. He finished himself. If he hadn't killed that drug smuggler, he'd end up by killing someone else. So this is what I told him and Dick Lake.

"It's no good thinking you can get rid of the body. If you took it to Fred Ayling's camp, he'd find a burial place so's it would never be found. But, in the first place, you wouldn't get it past Dick's home, for one of the children would hear the car, and you couldn't pass without stopping; and in the second place, we won't have Fred Ayling brought into it.

"In the buccaneers' cave you have skeleton keys of the lighthouse, so you told me a long, long time ago. One of you will fetch them keys. You'll drive the body to the Picnic Ground and carry it up to the lighthouse. It must be midnight now, and no one will be abroad this wet night. You'll strip the body naked—strip it of everything. You'll take the body into the lighthouse. It'll be two months before the next inspection's done, and if you plant it in the locker, it mightn't be found even then. You take everything belonging to the dead man to your old cave. No one has ever found that cave beside you boys, and no one is likely to now.

"Dick, he says it's a good plan and they'll carry it out. Eldred chips up like me and him is great friends, but I stops him quick. I tells him that when the body and the dead man's things are safely stowed, Dick drives him back to Geelong. Eldred is to keep travellin', to get as far away as he can, and keep away.

"Eldred wants to see his father and mother before leavin' Split Point. I tells him no. I tells him if he went home, or if he ever comes back, I'll tell the police about him. He tries to argue that if they plant the body like I said, and the clothes like I said, he could go home to see his parents. I tells Eldred that he takes it or leaves it, and Dick he tells Eldred that too. We don't argue with him, and Eldred says he'll do what we say.

"I runs over the plan again, and Dick says he's got it all clear. Dick's more himself now, more confident, but Eldred's snivelling, and I'm thinkin' Dick will have it all to do. In the dark, I hunted out some light rope, for no one could get down to the cave without havin' to use both hands. Without lightin' the lamp, I let 'em out, bided there five minutes, and went home. It was ten minutes after one."

The old man ceased speaking, and Bony significantly waited. Yet again Penwarden lit his pipe, and this time was calm enough to smoke. Bony completed the rolling of another cigarette before the old man proceeded.

"After that night I didn't see Dick for a week. In that week, of course, the inspector, coming down by chance, found the body. Murder will out, Mr. Rawlings, sir. I ought to have remembered that saying. Anyway, Dick came to tell me he'd driven Eldred to Ballarat, and Eldred had tipped a transport driver to take him across to Adelaide. And that's all."

"But how does Fred Ayling come into it?" Bony asked, and the old man sighed.

"Dick had to tell Fred. He'd never keep anything from him. Fred came here with Dick, to talk over what had been done with the dead man's clothes and luggage. Fred wanted Dick to fetch the things, and he'd take 'em back to his camp and destroy 'em properly. Not then, though. Not till after the detectives had given up and gone away. Dick backed me when I said they'd be safe enough where they were.

"But that wasn't so, Mr. Rawlings, sir. You found the cave. Mary Wessex seen you go down to it, and she told Fred about you and how she hit you with a rock. Fred told Dick and said he must bring up them clothes, if you'd of left them there. Didn't mean Dick to go to the cave when it was raining like it did that night. I didn't know anything about that till day afore yesterday. Fred came here to tell me, and saying that as you didn't look like a policeman you was an accomplice of the dead man come to ferrit out what happened to him."

"Did Mary Wessex know about the killing?"

"No. But she knew about the clothes and the case being in the cave. Unbeknownst to Dick, she went there sometimes. He happened to see her about to go down. You were on the beach that day, and he knew if she went down you would see her and guess there must be a cave. So he stopped her. Owen had come lookin' for Mary, and he was a bit too late to lend a hand."

Bony gazed hard into the now not so bright blue eyes, and slowly he asked:

"You are convinced that Eldred did not visit his parents—as you ordained?"

"Yes. Dick spoke true, and Eldred never came back after being taken to Ballarat."

"How do you account for the fact that the dead man's fingerprints were found on the handrail inside the lighthouse?"

"Dick said—Dick said, when he were tellin' me just what they done with the body, that as he were a-carrying it on his back up the steps, Eldred took holt of the dead man's hand and made his prints on the rail to sort of confuse things for when the body was found."

"To that extent, Eldred still had his wits."

"Seems like it were so," agreed Penwarden.

"It's certain that you had your wits about you that night. Tell me, what did you intend doing with my dead body inside the coffin?"

Penwarden slowly stood, the picture of bewilderment.

"Well, now . . . I don't rightly know, Mr. Rawlings, sir. I never got that far. You see, I didn't think what to do about you until you was being fitted."

Waited upon by the cheerful and tireless Mrs. Washfold, Bony lunched in solitary state. As Mrs. Washfold was inclined to linger beside his table, he asked her if Fred Ayling had returned to his camp, and was informed that the woodcutter was staying with the Wessexes.

"I never cottoned to him, Mr. Rawlings," she added. "Too moody for my liking. Up in the air one day and down in the dumps the next. Same with his ideas about you. One time praising you to the sky, and then crying you down. Don't mean anything, of course. Way he's made."

"I have sensed that peculiarity in him," Bony admitted. "What did he cry me down about?"

"Oh, you know how these country people can be—suspicious and all that. If they don't know just what you do and how much money you have in the bank, they imagine things. Never give credit to people for being natural. Fred can't understand why you have such an old car when you're a pastoralist and wool's over a hundred pounds a bale. Can't understand a man wanting to have a holiday in wintertime. Can't understand this and that, so has to imagine you're a detective, or a Russian spy, even a city gangster in smoke. Take no notice, Mr. Rawlings."

"Of course not, Mrs. Washfold. I must tell my wife about that. She'll say she wished I were a spy or a policeman and then I'd talk romantically instead of about wool and taxes."

After lunch he sat on the veranda and pondered on his next move. Penwarden had given him much that morning, and no man could be less unsophisticated and less prone to dissimulation. That Penwarden had spoken the truth, as he knew it, Bony believed, but doubted that the truth as known to Penwarden was all the truth.

The doubt was that Dick Lake had driven Eldred Wessex to Ballarat. Had he done so, had Eldred Wessex travelled as far distant as possible, why had Lake taken such risk to retrieve the clothes and suitcase, and why had Ayling told Penwarden that cock and-bull yarn that he, Bony, was an accomplice of the dead man? Were Eldred Wessex a thousand or ten thousand miles away, would it actually have mattered greatly that a detective had discovered the dead man's effects? The clothes and the contents of the suitcase had given little by comparison with that given by the death of Dick Lake.

Ayling had warned Penwarden not to gossip to the stranger Mr. Rawlings, and Ayling, who had served in the wartime Navy, would not be so simple as to think Bony was a criminal's accomplice. He had tried to influence the Washfolds against him, and had tried with less success to warn Moss Way. This action was more in keeping with the probability that Eldred Wessex was living somewhere on his father's farm, or beyond Sweet Fairy Ann with or near Fred Ayling.

Assuming this, it was unlikely that the fact would be conveyed to a friend and neighbour like Edward Penwarden, who already had done so much in cupboarding the skeleton of family dishonour.

Ayling was the next move.

As Ayling could be difficult, Bony sought Bert Washfold and told him he intended visiting Eli Wessex and would most certainly be back for dinner that night. He adopted a further unusual precaution of transferring from his suitcase to his pocket a small automatic.

Choosing to walk, Stug accompanied him.

Passing Penwarden's workshop, he observed that the door was shut—an interesting item, as it was then ten minutes after two. One hour after passing the workshop he rounded a bend in the track and came in sight of the road gate to the Wessex farm.

Outside the gate stood Ayling's old car. It was facing towards the hills and Sweet Fairy Ann. At the gate appeared Mary Wessex and Fred Ayling. Ayling carried a suitcase and, like a raincoat on his shoulder, several grey blankets.

Concealed by a tree, Bony watched Ayling pass the blankets and suitcase into the back of the car, go to the front and crank the engine. It was then obvious that the girl was disinclined to enter the car, resulting in a protracted discussion which terminated when

Ayling nodded assent. Whereupon the girl walked off the road and entered the forest opposite the farm, Ayling sitting on the running board and lighting a cigarette, clearly prepared to wait.

Bony waited too, keeping Stug with him. The suitcase was normal luggage for a man to bring from camp, but in view of the fact that Ayling habitually stayed with the Wessexes, he would not bring his own blankets.

After five or six minutes Mrs. Wessex appeared at the gate, and Ayling joined her. They talked for several minutes, when Mrs. Wessex returned to the house and Ayling to the car, and from the pantomime of their actions Bony was sure that Ayling had succeeded in quietening the woman's perturbation.

When the girl reappeared and stepped down the low bank to the road, she tiptoed to the car. Ayling caught her by the arm and without fuss put her into the front seat, and getting in behind the wheel, he drove off.

Bony smoked two cigarettes before he moved on.

Some time previously he had noted that where the girl had gone into the forest a truck had been driven in and out again, and he had thought the truck had been used for collecting firewood. On reaching this point, which was opposite the gate and in full view of the homestead, he, too, entered the forest.

The abnormal rain which fell on the night Dick Lake crashed to death had obliterated the track of the vehicle, but there were tracks made since that night by a woman's and a man's shoes size six—the shoes Mary Wessex had worn when she listened outside the door of the lighthouse, and again when she tiptoed to the veranda that afternoon Bony talked with her father. Prior to this afternoon the girl had entered the forest four times since the great rain. She had been alone.

Her tracks ended in a little dell shadowed by white gums and littered with flakes of limestone and windfalls from the trees. It was a pretty place even on this cold and windy day. Magpies were made angry by the intrusion, and small scarlet-capped brown finches twittered their alarm.

The girl had come here and stood about a long splinter of stone. There was nothing remarkable about the stone; for, as Bony had

179

noted, the floor of the dell was littered with these fragments of limestone. On her previous visits the girl had come to this particular fragment.

Walking back to the lip of the natural basin, he listened to the birds, watching them, tarried till assured no human was in the vicinity. On returning to the stone splinter, he turned it over.

Beneath, buried flush with the ground, was a small cedarwood box. He lifted the lid. The box contained a photograph of Eldred Wessex in a cheap metal frame and, within a dainty blue silk handkerchief, the fourth ring.

Returning the ring and the photograph, he put back the box and replaced the stone. To the dog who watched, he said:

"You will not come here again and dig up that box, Stug. Your load of fleas and my heaviness of heart are as nothing to the tragedy of that poor mind groping in the world of reality for a world she has lost, and finding no resting place in either. How blessed are we!"

Stug wagged his tail and followed Bony from the dell. Soberly the man returned to the road, and docilely the contented dog followed. They came to the Wessex farm gate, and there Bony leaned upon it and pensively regarded the neat homestead and the cleared paddocks beyond. No one was in view. Smoke slanted sharply from one of the three chimneys. Powerfully disinclined to open the gate, Bony did so and walked slowly to the house.

Mrs. Wessex answered his knock. There was no welcoming smile. The weather-ruined face held no expression, the voice no inflection.

"Please come in."

Eli Wessex sat between the window and the brightly burning fire. He was wearing a dressing gown, and his pathetic hands were resting uselessly in his lap. At Bony's entrance he neither looked up nor spoke, and it was his wife who invited the visitor to be seated at the other side of the fire. She drew forward a chair to sit between them.

"Mr. Penwarden telephoned that I was on my way?" asked Bony.

"He spoke to Fred Ayling," replied Mrs. Wessex dully, staring at the fire. "Fred told us. He's taken Mary away to the Lakes. They will look after her, and so will Fred. Fred has always loved her. You mustn't blame Fred for anything."

"Did Mr. Penwarden know that Eldred came home?"

The woman shook her head.

"I'm glad to hear that," he said. "Ayling knew that Eldred came home, stopped here?"

"Yes, Inspector. He got it all out of Dick." Abruptly she turned to him, a human being divested of its personality. "I am to blame for everything. Upon me is the mark. I am to blame for Eldred. And for Dick. I am to blame for dear old Mr. Penwarden, and for my husband."

Turning, she confronted the fire. Eli said nothing, nor did he move.

"I know already what was done about the killing of the man from Sydney," Bony said. "I know of Mr. Penwarden's contribution. Tell me how Eldred came to die."

"You found his grave?"

"Yes."

A long silence which Bony did not interrupt. When Mrs. Wessex spoke, Bony had to lean forward to hear what she said.

"We'd like you to know, Inspector Bonaparte, that we feel no animosity towards you. You are the agent of Nemesis, which we were silly enough to think we could escape. Had it not been you, it would have been another. Shall I tell him, Father, or will you?"

"You tell it, wife."

"We had only the one son, and we loved him above all else. I won't waste time by telling you about his boyhood, excepting to say he was lovable and impetuous, quick of temper and imaginative. You know all that. What I am going to tell you about Eldred we didn't know until the other day."

"Early in March," amended Eli.

"Early in March. Very early in the morning Eldred came home, and Dick Lake was with him. Eldred wanted to give us a surprise, and he did. He was much altered, for we hadn't seen him for eleven years, but there was something new about him we couldn't make out, and didn't try to at first.

"He told us he wanted to keep his visit a secret, even from the Owens, our near neighbours all our lives, and we didn't ask him why because we were so happy to have him home again. Dick went off to his camp about ten o'clock, and Eldred went to bed and stayed there all that day. That evening he told us how well he was doing in Sydney, and it was then that I thought the business was ruining his health and that I'd have to insist on his staying home so I could look after him.

"The next morning I heard about the murder. I happened to telephone to the grocer about an order, and he mentioned it. Naturally I wanted to hear more, and learned that if Mr. Fisher hadn't had to come down specially, the body mightn't have been discovered for months.

"Late that same day Dick came to see Eldred, who hadn't got up, and they were together for a long time. After Dick had gone, I went in to see Eldred. He looked awful. He was shaking all over, and he frightened me. When I said I would call the doctor, he shouted at me not to be a fool, as he was suffering only from a bout of malaria he'd got in the jungle.

"He told me to get him a glass of brandy. After I'd done that I took him a bowl of soup and some toast, as he said he wasn't hungry. Then he seemed better, but kept asking me if I'd told anyone he was at home. He'd already seen Mary, of course, but he was desperately anxious that she shouldn't say anything.

"A cold dread began to creep through me, he acted so strangely. I remembered that when Dick came with him in the early morning, and again that late afternoon, that he never once smiled as he always did. The dread in my mind I wouldn't face, not till Dick came again the next night.

"Dick brought brandy, three bottles of it, and he was with Eldred for more than an hour, Eldred still lying abed. It was about eleven when Dick went, and I walked with him to the road gate. At first he wouldn't tell me anything. I pleaded with him for some time; I mentioned Father, saying how worried he was about Eldred and that it couldn't go on. I've known Dick since he was a tiny tot, and I knew he would tell me eventually.

"When he'd told me everything, it was he who pacified me, and I came back to the house having agreed to do nothing and to say nothing.

"But I broke the agreement when I went in to Eldred after I'd put Father to bed. I told Eldred he would have to give himself up in the morning. He shouted that he would never do that. Then he laughed and told me I would see him sentenced to death, how I would live through the seconds when he would be put on the trap and hanged. He got out of bed and fell upon his knees, and implored me not to betray him.

"Then he boasted about his life in Sydney, the money he had made and how he had made it, how he had at first peddled cocaine and finally had taken it himself. He whimpered like a dog. He said he'd run out of the drug and that I'd have to get some somehow at Geelong. He got up and drank brandy from the bottle, and I didn't recognise him as Eldred. He—he wasn't a man any more.

"He said the man deserved what he got. He blamed him for everything, for smuggling drugs off the ship, for supplying him with other things he sold. He swore about Ed Penwarden suggesting what to do with the body, when they had the chance to take it over to Fred's camp.

"So it went on for hours, now and then Eldred drinking from the bottle, although there were already three glasses on the table by the bed. I thought of Father's sleeping tablets, and blamed myself for not thinking of them earlier. I fetched two and gave them to Eldred, and presently he fell asleep.

"That must have been near dawn. I sat on the foot of the bed looking at him. He lay comfortably on his back, one arm outflung, the other under the clothes. All the ugliness had gone from his face. He looked like he did when he went off to the war. He was my boy again. He was safe and asleep in his own room with the two pictures of ships under full canvas on the walls, and the text in the frame above the bed. After all the years, my empty heart was full again.

"When he woke he was just as bad as he'd been before. I said if he'd not give himself up, then the only thing to do was for Dick to drive him to Melbourne, anywhere to get away. He wouldn't hear of it, shouting that by now someone would have told the police

183

about him and the dead man in the lighthouse. I stayed with him most of that day until Dick came in the evening. Dick quieted him just a little, and when he left I went again with him to the road gate. He asked if I'd told Father about the murder, and I reminded him I'd never kept anything from Father. I begged him to think what we could do for Eldred, and Dick said there was nothing we could do except keep him full of brandy until the craving for cocaine passed off. Dick didn't sound hopeful, and then he told me that what Eldred was suffering from chiefly was fear. Said Eldred's way of living had rotted him, and fear was sending him insane.

"As I walked back to the house I thought of Mary, of all that Mary had suffered. I thought of Father, how wise he had been and how foolish I had been to override his views and advice. I thought of Mr. Penwarden, and what he had done to save Father and me and Dick. I thought of all that, was thinking of it as I went into Eldred's room.

"He was sitting on the side of the bed, the fingers of one hand clawing the side of his mouth, and his eyes glassy with fear and horror. I must have walked slowly to the door, for he shouted at me never to do that again, that I reminded him of the coming of the hangman.

"I said: 'You'll have to sleep, son. You must sleep!' So I went out to the kitchen and mixed him a sedative and took it to him, and he drank it.

"He became calmer, and finally he lay down and I lay with him and held him in my arms. All night long I held him, excepting once when I got up to put out the light. When he died . . . there was no struggle, just no more breathing. . . . I got up and went to Father and told him Eldred was dead."

There was silence. Eli Wessex, who had been so still that it could be thought he was dead, uttered one short sob. The woman's voice came again, thin, without tone, reminding Bony of the wind among the white gums surrounding the little dell in the forest.

"All my love for Eldred was wasted. There was nothing left in me to give but pity. In half a glass of brandy, I gave him ten of Father's tablets."

"And then you put Eldred in one of the coffins kept under your bed, and buried him in the forest beyond the road," Bony said as stating facts.

"In my coffin," whispered Eli.

"And Owen replaced the casket by having Penwarden make one ostensibly for Mrs. Owen."

"That was so."

Mrs. Wessex glanced at the clock on the mantel and stood. Saying nothing, she left the room. Old Eli's head drooped and his lean chin almost rested on his chest. In Bony sprang the urge for physical action that the depression on his mind might be relieved, but he remained quiescent. He was conscious of being trapped. He sought to identify the trap and found it. It was Napoleon Bonaparte, a detective inspector, a tiger cat that once on the trail never gives up, the personification of Victor Hugo's implacable trailer of men, Javert. It was the man who had never yet failed to finalise an investigation. That was the trap which closed about Bony, husband and proud father, the man of courage sufficient to conquer all those disabilities imposed by his ancestry, the man whose infinite patience was equalled by limitless sympathy.

Without thought for etiquette, he rolled and lit a cigarette. Sounds were emphasised—the hissing of a fire log, the clock, the movement of Mrs. Wessex in another part of the house. Then there occurred that which gave him one of the greatest shocks of his career. Mrs. Wessex came in with afternoon tea on a large tray. The one anchor to which she could cling in this time of catastrophe.

He placed a small table for her, and she poured the tea. As she had done that other afternoon when he was there, so did she raise the cup to her husband's lips. No one of them spoke until the woman had pushed the little table away and again sat between the two men.

"When Dick came that evening," she said, tonelessly as before, "I told him what I'd done. He went out and told Alfie to go for Mr. Owen. The three of them put Eldred in Father's coffin and carried it out to Mr. Owen's utility. I went with them. Mrs. Owen stayed to look after Mary and Father.

"We tried to keep it all from Mary, but it wasn't any use. She followed me to the truck, and we drove across the road and into the forest to the place where the children used to play. That was Dick's idea. Mary and I stood together while the men dug the grave. They were very careful to bring away all the earth displaced by the coffin and smooth away all traces.

"I never went back. Mary did. I used to watch her, but she was very good. We have tried, Father and I, to forget that time and remember only the years before Eldred went to the war."

Her voice trailed away to be captured by the ticking clock, the hissing logs. When Bony began the move to leave his chair, she said:

"I am ready to go with you, Inspector Bonaparte. I've packed a change of clothes."

With a swift rush and a cry like an agonised animal, the woman left her chair and fell upon her knees beside her husband. His hands went up to rest upon her head, the edges of the palms expressing what the locked and helpless fingers could not.

Bony crossed to the wall telephone. He asked Exchange for the Owens' number. When a woman answered the call, he asked for Tom Owen.

"I am speaking from the Wessex homestead," he said to Owen. "Would you and Mrs. Owen come over immediately? Mr. and Mrs. Wessex are in desperate need."

"Leave at once," came the prompt assent.

They arrived within fifteen minutes, to find Bony waiting on the veranda. The woman was concerned; the man grim.

"They are in the sitting room," Bony told Mrs. Owen. To her husband he said: "I have something to say before you go in." He paused to permit Mrs. Owen to leave them, before explaining who he was and giving a swift outline of his investigation. "That, Mr. Owen, is the complete tragedy, is it not?"

The man's grey eyes suddenly narrowed, and he nodded.

"That's about all of it."

"Now listen carefully. A man was done to death. He was a dope smuggler, among other things. The man who killed him was as bad. The world is well rid of both. The man who was the murderer's accomplice is also dead. Don't interrupt . . . Lake was Eldred's accomplice. The shadow of that crime has fallen on seven people, one of the seven being you. Another is old Penwarden.

"You know that Penwarden is aware only of part of the whole, that he does not know that Eldred came home, and all that followed. What Penwarden doesn't know, he must never know, but he must bear the responsibility for the advice he gave Dick Lake.

"Rightly or wrongly, I find I cannot censure Mrs. Wessex for what I, myself, would have done, and rightly or wrongly, I cannot censure you for what you did for them in their extremity. It is for you to guard the secret of the dell in the forest, and to control the minds, and thus the tongues, of those who share the secret with you. It is for me to continue the hunt for the murderer of Thomas Baker to Ballarat and beyond. Clear?"

Tom Owen tried to speak, gave it up, and nodded.

"Go in and comfort them," Bony said, and went down the veranda steps to pat the waiting Stug and walk slowly to the road.

Ed Penwarden was putting on his coat to go home when Bony entered the workshop, and his anxiety was not lessened when Bony swung shut the door and locked it.

"We have, Mr. Penwarden, a bone to pick," announced Bony slowly and coldly. "Make yourself easy. Tell me, why did you telephone to Fred Ayling, at the Wessex homestead, after I left you this morning?"

"Fred Ayling wasn't in it, Mr. Rawlings, sir." The old man sat stiffly upright on his packing case and looked steadily upward at Bony, who had drawn himself up on the bench. "You must believe that. He wasn't here when murder was done."

"Then why tell him I was on my way to question him?"

"I did no such thing. All I told him was that you'd found out about the murder and my part in telling Dick and Eldred what to do about it. I didn't know you were going along. I never saw you pass. All I said was for him to clear off back to his camp."

"Which he did," Bony said, and contemplated the creaseless face, the blue eyes, and the long white hair.

"Let him be, Mr. Rawlings, sir. He was allus a good lad, and he were terrible upset about Dick Lake. As Dick would say: 'I can take it.' Maybe in the eyes of the law I did wrong, but I'm not sorry. I wasn't thinkin' for Eldred, exceptin' he got well away from Split Point and his father and sainted mother, and from Dick Lake and all of us. You arrest me, and leave Fred out of it."

"What about your wife?"

"The old woman! Oh, she'll bide quiet till I come back."

Bony said:

"You may be away for ten years. Much too long for you to be away from Mrs. Penwarden. Like me, you are not normally a fool. Don't be a fool again, even although a fool is sometimes wise. I think it likely that my superiors will overlook you in their determination to catch up with Eldred Wessex. We will hope that he has left the country, or that he went to sea and was drowned. My work here is finalised. I found out who the dead man in the lighthouse was, and who killed him. It is for the Victorian police to find Eldred Wessex. Aided by science and wonderful organisation, I am confident that they will find him, perhaps in Adelaide, perhaps in London—anyway, far distant from Split Point."

He slipped off the bench, and Penwarden stood, saying:

"It would be grand, Mr. Rawlings, sir, if Eldred did get himself drowned-ed, or something happened so's his folk would never know what he did here."

"I agree," Bony said. "Now I must be off. I'll accompany you as far as your house. Don't worry about yourself, for it's unlikely you will be bothered by the police. Do we understand each other?"

A nobbly hand gripped Bony's forearm. A gleam of happiness sprang into the blue eyes, and Penwarden said earnestly:

"Seems like we've allus understood each other, Mr. Rawlings, sir."

They passed outside and Bony waited for the old man to lock up his workshop. Without haste, they walked towards the ancient's neat little house, the one upright and lithe, the other slightly stooped yet still sturdy on his feet.

"You'll not go back on acceptin' of the coffin, I hope," said the coffinmaker.

"Certainly not. I'll write giving my home address and nearest railway station—after you have written me what you think of the bloodwood logs. Police Headquarters, Brisbane, will always find me. And when I come again to Melbourne, I'll try to run down for a little gassing."

They shook hands. Bony smiled, his old beaming smile. Penwarden gave his deep-throated chuckle and they stopped outside his garden gate.

"Remember to take a shaving or two from the neck rest," Bony said. "I showed you just where the rest is a trifle uncomfortable."

He walked on, and Mr. Penwarden tarried at the gate to watch him until he reached the main road.

Enjoy these other exciting
Scribner Crime Classics, available at
your bookseller:

Arthur W. Upfield's
Inspector Napoleon Bonaparte mysteries

DEATH OF A LAKE
DEATH OF A SWAGMAN
THE DEVIL'S STEPS
MURDER DOWN UNDER
SINISTER STONES

S. S. Van Dine's Philo Vance mysteries

THE BENSON MURDER CASE
THE BISHOP MURDER CASE
THE "CANARY" MURDER CASE
THE GREENE MURDER CASE

Robert van Gulik's Judge Dee mysteries

THE EMPEROR'S PEARL
THE HAUNTED MONASTERY
JUDGE DEE AT WORK
THE LACQUER SCREEN
THE MONKEY AND THE TIGER
MURDER IN CANTON
NECKLACE AND CALABASH
PHANTOM OF THE TEMPLE
POETS AND MURDER
THE WILLOW PATTERN